CAMPFIRE TALES OF AN ERIE NATURE™

BRANDON HUMPHREYS

Edited by John Alvarado & Mical Pedriana

Artwork & Content

Copyright © 2015 Brandon Humphreys

All Rights Reserved.

www.ErieNature.com

ISBN-10: 1517658233

ISBN-13: 978-1517658236

For Mom

&

For Dad

CONTENTS

ACKNOWLEDGMENTS

E. Scot Humphreys

John Alvarado

Mical Pedriana

Helen Aberegg

Angel Kachenko & Joe Charboneau

Keith Arem

The crew at Inxile:

Matt Findley, Maxx Kaufman, Elene Campbell, Chris Keenan & Brian Fargo

Coast to Coast AM:

George Noory & George Knapp

Darkness Radio:

Dave Schrader & Tim Dennis

Chuck Schodowski & John Rinaldi

John Carpenter

R. L. Stine

&

Dean R. Koontz:

For an amazing letter of encouragement I've never forgotten.

Foreword:

This book is my tribute to the woods of northeast Ohio, a place I was fortunate to have grown up in. Early on, the forest was a special place of exploration and mystery, an area of rolling hills and unknown boundaries that provided fertile ground for an active imagination.

I invite you to visit the trails and parks of northeast Ohio.

But beware. Some of the events in this book actually happened.

CAMPFIRE TALES OF AN ERIE NATURE™

THE ROCKPILE

Paul and Jeremy had been friends since the start of summer. Jeremy's family had moved in up the street near the end of the school year, and once fifth grade let out, sheer proximity led the two to hang out often.

An unlikely duo, Paul would have probably spent more time indoors if Jeremy wasn't around. Jeremy brought him along to explore the new home construction down the street, shoot Jeremy's pellet guns in the nearby sand pits, or hunt frogs in the nearby creeks. Unlikely to approve if they knew of these 'risky' activities, Paul's parents were happy, however, to see he had a neighborhood friend that finally got him active and out of the house.

While Jeremy seemed to have more expensive toys and less parental rules, Paul was particularly jealous of Jeremy's lack of a curfew. Especially during summer, having to be home for supper at six o'clock really cut into his 'play' time. If he ate quickly and was courteous to his parents, he could get back outside for a few more hours before the sun set. At this latitude and time of year, the dusk stretched out just past 9pm, which was his final 'get home or get grounded' time.

Earlier Paul had ridden his bike down to Jeremy's house, stopping to knock on the door, though there was no answer. Passing by the creek on his way home, he found plenty to investigate in the nearby creek and banks. He spotted and captured several crayfish and even a few salamanders, but with no good container, released each shortly thereafter.

After finishing supper, Paul was climbing a tree in his backyard when he saw Jeremy come through the treeline. He explained to Paul how he had been wandering around the fields after fishing this morning and had ventured into the nearby woods. There were plenty of woods close by that Paul and Jeremy had explored, but this stand was outside of their usual adventures, owing to Paul not being much of a fisherman, leaving Jeremy to fish alone.

Jeremy described coming across a huge pile of rocks within the trees that Paul had to see, describing it as "probably the remains of a castle!" Paul was intrigued, and Jeremy assured him they could get out there to check it out further before it got too dark.

Paul quickly ran to the garage and grabbed a small knapsack he always carried on their larger explorations, filled with a penknife, two cans of soda, a spool of kite string, and a military surplus shovel his dad never seemed to miss. He also grabbed a yellow plastic flashlight, a pack of matches and a few sparklers left over from the Fourth of July, and stuffed them into his bag.

As Paul ran towards the treeline with Jeremy he heard his mother call out from inside the house "Don't be home late!" They made their way past the treeline and through the overgrown field beyond. They followed the trail bordering the local forest and past a swamp. Almost an hour later, they reached the lake Jeremy had been fishing at earlier. At this point the sun was starting to dip in the sky and the surroundings had begun to take on a golden hue.

Jeremy led Paul into the unfamiliar forest, and the two wandered around briefly attempting to relocate the rockpile.

"It's got to be around here somewhere," exclaimed a perplexed Jeremy, running down into the small valley and up the hill opposite. Paul began to have second thoughts about tonight's adventure, and he thought perhaps Jeremy might be pulling his leg. From another hilltop within the forest, Jeremy finally called out to Paul, "Here it is!"

Paul quickly made his way over to the next hill, forgetting about his earlier doubt. Sure enough, on the next rise sat a pile of rocks that must have been ten feet tall, the base twice as wide, with each boulder larger than a cantaloupe. Moss and debris littered the edges, but the pile was certainly not something Mother Nature had placed. "What do you think it is?" Paul asked Jeremy.

"I told you already, it's probably from an old castle, or fort," Jeremy replied, already scrambling up the pile.

"I'd be careful, it doesn't look safe," warned Paul.

"Don't be such a whiner — hey!" Jeremy froze.

"What is it? A rattlesnake?" Paul asked, reaching for his shovel.

"No, a coin!" Jeremy replied, and rubbed a dirty disc between his fingers. Paul's apprehension was overtaken by his curiosity and he scaled up the pile.

"Lemme see," Jeremy held out the piece for Paul to examine.

Sure enough, edges of silvery metal shone through the grime, and Paul could make out a vague profile. Paul knew some coins, as his grandfather had a small collection he would share with Paul when they would visit his grandparents' house. But he didn't recognize this

3

coin. "This must be really old!" Paul exclaimed as Jeremy snatched the coin.

"This one's mine, but I'll bet there's plenty more underneath - help me move some of these of these rocks!" Jeremy said as he pocketed the coin.

Jeremy put his weight behind one of the topmost rocks and pushed, the rock bouncing down the side of the rockpile. Just then Paul felt a breeze. And he finally noticed how low the sun had sunk, and how the golden glow had begun to fade. "I don't know, maybe we ought to get going," Paul offered, stepping down the rocks of the pile.

"Are you kidding, we just found a coin and you want to leave?" Jeremy countered.

"Well, it is getting late and I don't want to get grounded... besides what if it's like... an indian burial ground or something?" Paul shuddered.

"Sheesh! Are you kidding Paul? Are you gonna help me move these rocks or what?" Jeremy struggled with the second rock, sending it tumbling to the base of the pile. Paul noticed the warm light had completely faded with the setting of the sun and was replaced with a blueish cast. He also noticed the breeze seem to pick up, at least on the back of his neck.

"Let's come back tomorrow when there's more light, and I'll help you move all the rocks, Jeremy," Paul said, as he looked around at the dimming woods. He fished the flashlight out of his backpack and switched it on, shining the faint beam up towards Jeremy.

Jeremy stared down at Paul. "Look, if you're gonna be a wuss, go on home. But leave the flashlight." Paul considered his options, switched off the light, stepped up and handed the yellow flashlight to Jeremy.

Paul immediately knew he had disappointed Jeremy. He considered staying just a little longer, then thought of his parents wrath if he came home late. If he hurried, he might still be able to get home on time. "Ok, sorry, I just don't want to get in trouble with my folks," he partially lied, as the place was really starting to creep him out.

"Yeah, whatever," Jeremy muttered as he pushed another rock down the side of the pile.

Paul apprehensively started back the way they had come, slightly unsure of the location of the lake. "Maybe this wasn't such a good idea," he whispered, and looking back towards the now distant rockpile, he saw the light of the flashlight switch on and illuminate the trees surrounding the rockpile.

Paul found his way to the lake with much relief, and jogged the trails through the fields and along the treelines back towards his house. Before he passed by the swamp he paused to light a few sparklers, which did little to ward off the shadows. He wished for the flashlight, then thought of how Jeremy might not even want to be his friend anymore. He noticed the stars in the darkening sky, and the chirping of the crickets as his sparklers fizzled out. Fortunately his house was within sight, up the trail and past the treeline.

He reached for another sparkler and struck a match against the back of the matchbook, and as soon as it flared up, a sudden breeze extinguished it. Paul quickly tore off another match, then noticed the crickets had stopped chirping. In fact the field and nearby forest were still, and Paul thought he should have heard the breeze rustling the leaves, at least a little, but there was only silence.

The hairs stood up on the back of his neck. He struck the match. It flared and burned, and Paul hesitated briefly, but before he could bring it to the sparkler,

it was blown out.

Paul immediately freaked as his flight instinct kicked in, and he ran for his house faster than he had ever run in his life.

Arriving home just as his curfew came and between gulps of air, Paul explained to his parents where he had been. After a few admonishments about being out near dark and in the woods, his mother promised cookies after he helped with the dishes, with his father quickly enlisting him as the designated dish dryer. An exhausted Paul later fell asleep.

The next day caused a brief stir as Jeremy's mother came to Paul's house looking for her son, who hadn't returned last night. As Paul began to see the panic in Jeremy's mother, he began to worry as well. His concern was short-lived however, as Jeremy's father pulled up in a car honking, and after Jeremy's mother ran out and left in the car, his mother related something about a police officer finding Jeremy walking home.

He didn't see much of Jeremy the rest of that summer. When he visited his house no one answered, until one time his mother answered the door. She told Paul sternly that Jeremy was not available, whatever that meant. Later that year Paul passed by their house and saw a realty sign in the yard. It was clear Jeremy's family had moved away.

Many years later Paul ran into a former classmate, and as they were catching up, mention was made of a kid who briefly attended their school, who then killed some people as a minor and was institutionalized. Now a journalism student in his final year of college, Paul was able to track down that it was indeed his friend Jeremy from so many years ago, and that he had somehow caused the death of his parents while they slept.

During a subsequent visit home with his parents, the subject came up, and so too did the rockpile. His father, who was friends with a few local police officers, told him the property had been cleared years prior to make way for a housing development, but that it had caused a delay in construction and briefly was talk of the town as the skeleton of a boy had been found buried underneath the many tons of rocks.

The police investigated and declared the remains to be ancient. Native American archeologists were then contacted, but they declared it to be insignificant, as recent objects had been found with the skeleton.

Specifically, a yellow flashlight, and a pair of jeans with a coin in the pocket.

Returning to his apartment, his answering machine held a warning from Paul's classmate:

'Jeremy' was soon to be released.

THE WITCH HOUSE

Danny watched the clock; it was only minutes from lunch, and his stomach was growling. He saw the second hand appear to move slower the more he watched. He had finished his math quiz early and was daydreaming about what might be served in the cafeteria today. He was hoping for pizza when the teacher's voice interrupted his thoughts, as she called for the quizzes to be passed forward and collected.

Papers collected, the bell finally rang, and Danny lifted up his desk top to deposit his pencil, and take out his collection of small monsters. They weren't real monsters of course, but three brightly colored rubber toy creatures he had gotten from a vending machine several weeks ago. The monsters accompanied him wherever he went as of late, and he stuffed them in his corduroy pockets.

Danny got in line as his class exited their second grade homeroom and began the trip up the hall to the Cafeteria. Danny made a stop at the restroom, washing his hands like his mother had taught him before eating. Several other boys from his class also stopped at the restroom, but few of them actually remembered to wash up. A pair of fraternal twins, John and Joey, did remember to wash up. They were talking about lunch, and both agreed they hoped it was not a pizza day.

Danny followed the twins into the lunch line, collected his fiberglass tray and was slightly disappointed at what was served onto his plate, something that was described as a chicken casserole, with green beans and a biscuit, and a chocolate cookie. The cookie almost made up for the lack of pizza, Danny thought, as he added a small carton of milk to his tray.

Entering the crowded cafeteria, he found a seat at the end of the bench closest to the wall, far enough away to not be teased if he took his monsters out, which he set on the bench beside him. Danny's parents had moved over the summer, and only a month and a half into the new year at the new school, Danny was not easily making friends. Everyone seemed to know one another already, and Danny could easily be described as a shy kid.

After lunch came recess, and Danny rushed out with the rest of the kids to the playground at the back of the school. He liked this playground; there was a lot of equipment here compared to his old school; two kinds of monkey bars, a large set of swings, merry-go-rounds, see-saws and something called an ocean-wave. Most of the kids had congregated to play a game of kickball, and the twins asked Danny if he wanted to play, but he shook his head as he headed to the swings.

With a rubber seat and long metal chains reaching high above, this swing set was how Danny spent most of his recesses. He had a vague notion of one day attempting to swing so high and fast that he could do a loop, but wasn't entirely sure if that was possible. He knew he'd have to practice. As he swung, he surveyed the schoolyard, the baseball area, and the large fields where the older kids played soccer and football in. Beyond the play areas, stood the tall grass of the surrounding fields, and those edges were off limits.

Policing those boundaries were the recess monitors, several older volunteer women who made sure no one got into fights, wandered off, or got into any other mischief. They were evenly dispersed amongst the playground in their bright orange safety vests, and one walked by as Danny swung back and forth.

Further out beyond the overgrown fields was the edge of a forest that seemed to stretch from horizon to horizon, gently sloping hills covered with old growth trees of all varieties. The colors of Autumn had just begun to show, and to Danny, it was a colorful wilderness beyond.

Danny had been focused on the swing for a little over a week, and he found that he liked being away from the majority of the kids for the recess. Most of the children were engaged in kickball and an impromptu touch football game, while others huddled in social groups talking near the school building. There were few others using the equipment as the warmer temperatures were starting to fade, at least until winter arrived and gloves became the norm.

A girl Danny had seen for the last week around the playground approached and took the swing adjacent. She wasn't in his class, and he didn't know her name. But she seemed nice and smiled at him when he looked her way. She began swinging, kicking her legs, gradually building momentum. Danny was impressed, a girl who seemed to like swinging as much as he did. Eventually the bell rang, signaling an end to recess, and they both stopped to return to class.

"What's your name? I'm Danny," he said as they walked hurriedly back.

"Hi Danny. My name is Stephanie," she replied.

"Maybe I'll see you tomorrow," Danny responded, almost as a question. Stephanie smiled again, and as they filed on into the school, Danny found he couldn't wait for tomorrow's recess to arrive.

Tomorrow was pizza day, and the twins were as unhappy as might be expected. Danny was halfway through lunch when he remembered he had left his monsters inside his desk. He was thinking about the swings and wondering if Stephanie would be there. He figured the monsters wouldn't mind a day off.

When Danny made it to the giant swing set Stephanie was already there swinging, and he took his usual seat nearby. She smiled again as he swung back and forth, and soon Danny was up to speed. After about ten minutes Stephanie slowed down, and remained seated. Danny slowly stopped as well. The sky was full of clouds, though only some seemed thick enough to blot out any light. Their shadows moved across the fields, and the woods beyond.

"What's the matter, don't ya want to swing?" Danny asked. One of the recess monitors walked nearby, and they both stared at her until she had walked on.

"I think I can see it." Stephanie squinted towards the woods. Danny followed her gaze and looked where she was facing, but saw nothing but forest and sky.

"See it… See what?" he asked, and cupped a hand over his eyes as a visor. He had seen his father do this when looking at something intently.

"Out there, you don't see it?" She pointed with her finger towards the rolling hills of forest.

Danny peered again in earnest. "All I see is a bunch of trees. Maybe I need glasses?" Danny saw other kids in school with glasses and wanted a pair, but a trip to the eye doctor said they were unnecessary.

"Well it's kind of a secret, but it's what I heard from some of the other kids. Can you keep a secret?" Stephanie asked, glancing over at him.

"Um, yeah I think so," he said.

"Alright, cool. Now look out there where I'm pointing," she said. Danny followed her direction once more and squinted with additional effort. "Way out there, up in those hills, that house, do you see it?" she asked.

Danny scanned the area, as far as he could see to the fuzzy edge of the sky meeting the forest, but all he saw was trees. He wondered if he could see as far as her, and didn't want to disappoint her by not seeing it. He thought perhaps his eyes could only see so far, and had no idea how far away he was supposed to be looking. It was the first time he had thought about the edge of his vision, and how far away the horizon really was.

"I think so. Maybe?" Danny guessed. "What about it?"

Stephanie took a deep breath. "I heard from the other kids, that way up there in those hills is an old woman's house. More of an old shack, really. Some of the kids called her... a witch," she whispered.

"A witch?" Danny scrunched up his nose. He knew about witches from Halloween, which was still a month away, with their pointed hats and brooms. Danny clenched up his eyes further to try and see the house of this witch. The end of recess bell rang, and they made their way back.

Over the next few days Danny met Stephanie again by the swings, and they swung for awhile and talked briefly about other things, but the topic eventually returned to the house in the hills, the house of the witch. Danny scanned the horizon repeatedly, and he would ask her to describe the roof. He wanted to walk further out to the edge of the field to get a better look, but one of the recess monitors kept lurking around, the same from before. He had heard another kid in the playground call her Miss Tegkwitz.

Danny was starting to be unsettled by the woman, and would change the subject when she walked nearby. "That woman keeps watching us," Danny said to Stephanie in a hushed tone.

"Yeah, she is starting to give me the creeps too. I bet she smells." Stephanie chuckled, and Danny laughed uneasily. Miss Tegkwitz was farther away now, but cast a quick glance back their way.

The wind was starting to pick up, and a few leaves were beginning to blow across the grounds, no doubt fallen from the distant forest that held their attention. "You know what?" Stephanie asked.

"What?" Danny said.

"We should walk out to the field, and try to get a closer look," Stephanie proposed.

"Maybe…" Danny mulled the idea over in his head.

"I would go alone, but… I'd feel braver if you came with me," Stephanie said as she smiled at Danny.

"Well, we'd have to go when Miss Tegkwitz wasn't looking. She's one of the guards, and they never let anyone go near the edge of the field," Danny explained.

"Maybe if we go when she isn't looking, after she passes back the next time, I'll bet we could make it without her noticing," Stephanie proposed.

"Maybe. But it seems like she watches us more as recess goes on. We should try to go first thing tomorrow, right as all the kids are running out," Danny suggested.

"Yeah, that sounds like a good idea. Tomorrow," she agreed.

The next day Danny found himself watching the clock again,

counting down the minutes until lunch, and then recess. He was surprised when an aide came to the room, and after a brief conversation with his teacher, his teacher asked him to accompany the aide. Danny was led down the halls towards the administration and principal's office, and started to worry that he was in trouble. He had never been in those offices, and was surprised again to see his mother in the front office. Danny entered, and his mother gave him a hug.

The principal's door opened, and inside was the principal, Mr. Wright, a tall imposing man, and Miss Tegkwitz was in the room with him. The woman eyed Danny eerily, and he at once wondered if she, Miss Tegkwitz, wasn't actually a recess monitor, but the one who lives in the woods — the witch. He shuddered, and his mother directed him to stay on the seats outside while she went into the principal's office, with the principal and Miss Tegkwitz. Danny fidgeted uneasily, and occasionally looked up at the aide who was fussing with some paperwork behind the array of desks and counters.

Through the door he could hear their voices, sometimes raised, when he finally heard Mr. Wright exclaim: "I'm sorry, but Miss Tegkwitz has seen it. During recess, your boy has been talking to himself for the last week."

WOODHOLLOW

Jerry pedaled his bike around the corner, pumping the pedals harder as the street sloped upward. He rode to the next house on the right, and pulled into their driveway, absent of cars. From within the canvas satchel wrapped around his handlebars, he withdrew a folded copy of the Record Journal and placed it just inside the front screen door. The Bliss's, the only home on this stretch of street he had to deliver to, was almost at the apex of his delivery route.

The first half of his route contained a number of the more recent homes, homes that were built with smaller yards. As a result he was able to unload about two thirds of his papers before being half-way through his route. The remaining customers continued on up Briar Street, before his loop ultimately brought him to Hemlock drive and the final customers on the way to home.

Before he could get to Briar street however, he had to take Woodhollow street, a half mile stretch of country road that only had one driveway along it, for a house set far back from the road. Jerry thought he had spotted it once earlier in the Spring before the leaves had filled in, but with all of the trees on the property it was hard to be sure. Several of his friends from the neighborhood had told him about there being a 'spook house' out on Woodhollow, and that was good for a few nervous laughs whenever anyone would make a dare to visit; dares that were only half-heartedly made and never followed through on.

He thought about those friends, most were probably off playing football or over at Timothy's house, who had recently gotten a Colecovision game system. It was far better than the Atari, or so he had heard. Ever since taking on the paper delivery job, Jerry had a lot less time for play, and he seemed to only see his neighborhood friends in passing at school. Delivering newspapers took up almost two hours after school each day, a few more on the weekends, and then several more collecting subscription money on Thursday, Friday and Saturday.

Still he liked the money he was making, every other Saturday he would head down to the News and Tobacco shop with his dad and pick up a handful of comic books and a candy bar. It made him feel good to not have to ask his dad for 'toy' money. His dad would remind him to try to save as much as he spent, for what he called a 'rainy day fund'.

The clouds overhead were threatening to make it a rainy day of a different sort as Jerry finished the last of the deliveries along Briar Street before turning onto Woodhollow. This was an older part of the county, an uneven road that was not maintained as well as the others along his route. Few of the surrounding residents used the road, taking the trip along this route was only convenient for Jerry's delivery loop.

On Sunday mornings, one of his parents would drive him around his route with the Monte Carlo trunk filled with papers. Jerry would walk the paper to each door. One Sunday while driving the loop with his dad he asked about the Woodhollow area, and his dad mentioned something about it being some 'old timer' who owned most of the land along the street and for many acres beyond.

The wind rustled the tall maples along Woodhollow, and Jerry thought he felt a small raindrop hit the back of his neck. He had delivered several times in a drizzle before, but not a full rain, and certainly not a downpour. He pedaled faster and dodged a pothole as he felt another drop.

The sky seemed to darken as he approached the driveway, and a gust pushed hard against him, slowing his momentum. He glanced at the house to his left as he pedaled harder, hoping to regain some speed, and heard a sharp squealing noise from the direction of the house. Whatever it was, Jerry looked quickly away, having no interest in finding the source of the noise. Jerry quickly put the house behind him as he thought he heard another shriek.

About an hour later the he returned home having avoided any showers, though the sky hadn't cleared any. He briefly wondered if he had forgotten anyone, as he still had an extra paper in his delivery bag, though he wasn't too alarmed as the paper count was often off by a few. At least he wasn't short, otherwise he'd have to 'sacrifice' his own family's paper or head off to the corner store to purchase the few he was short. Jerry felt an obligation to make sure his customers got their paper each day.

As he neared his driveway, he stopped to check the mailbox. Today was the day his paper bill came, along with any supplemental information from the newspaper. There was an additional envelope with his bill, and he headed inside, after setting the kickstand on his bike out front.

His mom greeted him and pointed out some pecan and blueberry chip cookies she had baked earlier, which he quickly munched on. Brushing aside cookie crumbs from the envelope he opened the letter. It was a new subscription notice, set to begin today:

1 Woodhollow Drive. Jerry gulped and briefly forgot the half eaten cookie in his hand. He jumped when his mother set down a glass of milk in front of him. She asked if everything was ok, and he lied so she wouldn't worry, but he quickly began dreaming up reasons he shouldn't deliver the final leftover paper.

Usually he walked papers to the doorstep, but perhaps he could make an exception here and just throw this one down the driveway. Surely the customer, whose name didn't appear in the letter, would quickly cancel if they received poor service. Especially if the paper was soggy. Yes, that would be the plan, and he drank most of his glass of milk.

Jerry found himself pedalling up Woodhollow drive again, earlier than he would have liked, but the sooner the task was completed the better. The clouds appeared to darken again as he neared the driveway and stopped to reach in his bag. He finally got a good look up the crooked driveway, and he could see the old house well for the first time. It was a multi-story structure with a covered porch that resembled none of the other houses in the area. He cocked his arm ready to chuck the paper up the driveway, then heard the shriek once more.

But this time he spotted the source of the noise. Atop the aged structure was an old weather vane, and Jerry saw it rotate with the wind, its base clearly in need of a good oiling. He suddenly felt foolish for having been afraid earlier.

He surveyed the house with its peeling paint, overgrown yard, and ancient rusting cars parked adjacent to the house. Beyond he could see another structure behind the house, as well as a barn further back. Suddenly the house didn't appear quite as spooky as it had in his mind. He decided that leaving the paper in the driveway wasn't the right thing to do, and he began walking his bike slowly up the overgrown driveway.

He set his bike down and walked over some step-stones to the small front porch and stepped onto the wooden platform, which creaked underfoot. There was no screen door like most of the other houses, and there were some wet patches on the porch, so he folded the paper and wedged it between the doorknob and door jam. He turned to leave the porch and instantly heard scratching from behind the front door.

Alarmed, Jerry attempted to tiptoe off the porch, but the boards were not cooperative and issued a groan. The scratching suddenly turned to a low guttural growl. Jerry scrambled for his bike, running it up the driveway before frantically hopping on and pedalling out onto Woodhollow drive as fast as he could pedal.

He delivered the paper the rest of the week with no further incidents, though didn't let his guard down when leaving the paper. When collecting day came around, Jerry was prepared. He had a handful of dog biscuits in his jacket pocket in case the beast behind the door got loose. The dog biscuit trick worked on two other dogs at a home on Briar Street.

He rang the doorbell, but heard no sound. Perhaps it no longer worked, so he tried it again before half-heartedly knocking. Still nothing. Not even the scratching. Satisfied to delay any encounter, he turned towards his bike, and —

jumped. Standing in the way was an old man. He looked older than Jerry's grandfather and about as grizzled and weathered as anyone he had ever seen. "You must be the paperboy. I'm Elias Woodhollow. Don't worry about my dog. He's asleep." He extended a knobby and gnarled hand. Jerry remembered his manners, and shook Mr. Woodhollow's hand. "Good handshake, boy. Now what do they call you?" He squinted at Jerry.

"I'm - I'm Jerry… I'm, uh, collecting for the paper. $1.70."

Mr. Woodhollow smiled, and put his hand into his pocket and fished out a handful of coins, sorted out a few and handed the silver to Jerry. "That enough? My eyes aren't as good as they used to be." Jerry opened his hand and looked at the collection of coins, several dollar and half dollar coins, more than twice what was owed. He kept two of the dollar coins, then pushed three dimes from his change maker.

"A little too much, sir," Jerry handed the surplus coins back.

Mr. Woodhollow's squint turned to a smile. "You do a good job, Jerry. And you're an honest young man too." He handed Jerry back a fifty cent coin. "This is for not letting my paper get wet." Jerry smiled, and Mr. Woodhollow stepped out of the way of his bike.

"Thank you, sir," Jerry replied, and mounted his bike.

"Jerry - I've got some yardwork I could use some help with." He motioned to the lawn, full of leaves, branches and dead weeds. "The pay is five dollars an hour. Think it over."

"Ok, I will," Jerry replied and began pedalling towards the road named after the man he had just met.

After discussing the matter with his parents, Jerry soon began doing yardwork for Mr. Woodhollow, raking leaves, collecting branches, pulling weeds. When winter came, he shoveled the driveway, and when spring came along, he mowed the large yard with an old push mower from the shack behind the Woodhollow house. Occasionally they would chat when Jerry got paid each week, and Mr. Woodhollow always made him promise to save at least half of his earnings.

That summer Jerry asked Mr. Woodhollow if he wanted to clean up the back yard as well, and how far in back he should mow. The old man was feeling up for a walk, and with a cane in hand, took Jerry on a tour of the back perimeter. They walked to a spot about half an acre behind the house and an old barn, and Jerry stared at the woods beyond and asked how far back his property went.

"Well, It's been a long time anyone has asked me that, but a little over three hundred acres."

"Wow," Jerry uttered.

Then Mr. Woodhollow corrected himself, "That's not right - It's over three thousand acres." Jerry gasped, and wondered exactly how big an acre was.

"I'm kind of glad you don't need that mowed. Do you ever go out there?" Jerry asked.

"Not nearly as often as I used to. Once I knew every inch, used to hunt and fish and learned all about the outdoors from my daddy." Mr. Woodhollow's voice trailed off in memory. "Jerry, how much do you know about the woods?"

"I know a little… I like to climb trees and stuff." Jerry shrugged.

"Well, there's a lot more to forests than just trees. I think the mowing can wait. Let's go for a hike." Mr. Woodhollow hobbled forward with his cane down an overgrown path towards the distant treeline. Jerry was surprised at how active Mr. Woodhollow was, and he decided to follow him down the trail.

Over that summer Jerry spent most of his time in the woods going on short hikes with Mr. Woodhollow, learning all about the various plants, roots and seeds that could be harvested and eaten, how to spot and identify animal tracks, and how to move quietly through the woods to sneak up on deer or the wild turkeys roaming the forest. When the mosquitoes got too heavy, Mr. Woodhollow lit up an old cigar and puffed heartily, driving away the airborne vermin.

Mr. Woodhollow seemed to benefit both from the regular exercise and from the sharing of old knowledge his father had shown him.

With each hike they seemed to venture a little deeper into the woods, and Jerry learned plenty. When they passed streams, Mr. Woodhollow showed him how to spot the hideouts of newts, salamanders and crawdads, to appreciate the carpets of wild onions called Ramps growing on the forest floor, and when they neared the swamps, he showed Jerry several uses for cattails, including how to make a crude torch.

When they passed stinky bogs, Mr. WoodHollow pointed out Skunk Cabbage and how to avoid losing a shoe in the 'soggy bottoms' as he called them, which made Jerry laugh. Mr. Woodhollow also laughed, but warned Jerry to take the bogs seriously, as they could be dangerous if not paying attention, and he related the tale of an outlaw on the run supposedly swallowed up by one.

As summer gave way to autumn, and after Jerry had finished raking the front yard, he and Mr. Woodhollow took their longest walk yet. Jerry had never really noticed the posts and rusty barbed wire that lined the property on the street until recently. Mr. Woodhollow had mentioned that he and his father had put up the original fencing a long time ago, back in the late twenties.

As they crested a small hill, Jerry pointed out a decaying wooden fence that seemed to enclose a vast overgrown mound, surrounded by dense trees. Mr. Woodhollow stood transfixed, and Jerry was unable to read the emotions contorting Mr. Woodhollows face. "What is it? Are you Ok?" Jerry was concerned. Mr. Woodhollow regained his composure, and with a sigh, suggested they turn back as he was getting tired. Jerry acquiesced, and they walked back to the house through the dense woods, leaves falling around them.

When they returned Mr. Woodhollow sat on a chair on the back porch, and Jerry leaned against a post while seated on the stairs. Jerry studied Mr. Woodhollow's face, while he fiddled with a pipe. "That fence wasn't the edge of your property, was it? Jerry inquired.

"No. No it wasn't Jerry." Mr. Woodhollow set down the pipe and focused on Jerry. "I suppose I better tell you what that's all about or curiosity will get the better of you." The old man's eyes narrowed. "But if I do, you need to promise not to go out there, go inside that wooden fence." Jerry nodded in agreement.

Mr. Woodhollow lit his pipe, puffing several times. "It has been so long since I had been out there, I had forgotten exactly where it was. My father and I used to walk all over those woods, but I probably haven't been back there for over forty... fifty? ...years. Not since we put up the fence." Mr. Woodhollow's voice became a whisper. Jerry shifted, and looked back towards the woods.

"Years ago things were different, there was this thing called... Prohibition, when the authorities made it illegal for us common folk to drink whiskey and other such spirits. Well, my father was never one to listen to the 'authorities', and built a still near a little cave. Do you know what that is?" Jerry nodded, he had seen an episode of an old TV show where a sheriff broke apart a still.

"Did the police catch him?" Jerry asked.

"No, the local law at the time wasn't terribly concerned. They kind of looked the other way if you shared and didn't make a lot of money. My father made it for himself and his friends, friends who had wives, wives who went to a Baptist church that used to be near the center of town." Mr. Woodhollow motioned off to the west.

"Everything was fine for a few years into the ban. I remember helping bring corn out to the still with my daddy, learning how to make 'firewater'." Mr. Woodhollow chuckled.

"Like moonshine!" Jerry offered. Mr. Woodhollow nodded in agreement.

"Like moonshine. But one day the church got a new pastor, a southern fellow spouting fire and brimstone about the evils of...

moonshine. He even had a fancy leather bible he carried around with him everywhere. Well, he got those wives whipped into a frenzy, and soon the rest of the town, about how the 'scourge' of alcohol needed to be wiped out."

Mr. Woodhollow re-lit his pipe with a wooden match. "One of my daddy's friends was pressured to disclose the location of the still, and soon there was a regular witch-hunt of church-goers following this pastor deep into those woods." Mr. Woodhollow motioned beyond the treeline.

"My daddy was away in a field when they went in, but came home shortly after, and went after them to chase them off this property. He told me to stay here, but I snuck after him anyhow, thinking I might help in some way. When my father caught up with them they had already found the still, and he belted his friend in the jaw but good. Several of the fervent got hold of him, and the pastor began a sermon, reading from his book, while the 'faithful' took axes to my daddy's still."

Mr. Woodhollow's voice trailed off and his eyes glazed as the memories unfolded. "Had I brought a gun I would have..." He caught himself, and resumed. "I had been to church with my parents early on and I have read the Bible since, but what the pastor read over that still was not from any Bible I've ever heard of. Most of it wasn't even english.

"Shortly thereafter, the sky opened up, wind and sheets of rain drove them out, and I barely made it back to the house before my daddy did. I thought sure he would catch me with muddy feet and wet clothes, but he didn't seem to notice. I imagine he was rather... preoccupied.

"It wasn't too long afterwards that the pastor was revealed to be a phony, a huckster from the south who was stealing from the church. My father and a few of his friends were the ones who uncovered him, and before they drove him out of town he admitted to many things, including that his so called Bible had been stolen from a museum overseas. They said he headed northeast. Though the next town was apparently not so forgiving, as their church burned to the ground with him in it.

"Soon after the hysteria died down, my daddy went back to try and rebuild his still one day while I was in school. When I came home he looked quite shaken, and made me swear to never go near the site, and said that he was going to put a fence up that I was never to cross. And I never have."

Mr. Woodhollow's gaze shifted downward as he admitted: "Except once. That next year I did get curious, and by then he had built that wooden fence around the whole area, larger than an acre. I figured there was a lot of sharp metal and broken glass, maybe something poisonous he didn't want me to mess with, but I climbed that fence late one afternoon.

"As I got close to the rock up top, I could see movement but I couldn't make out what it was. Whatever it was, it was big, and it must have seen me. I never ran so fast in my life since, and only by climbing high into a tree did I stay on this Earth. The sun set and I was there all night, positive that whatever it was, was waiting for me on the ground. It was noon the next day before I climbed out of that tree, and I was tired and sore, and got a licking when I got home, though I lied about where I had been all night. I worried that had I told my father the truth, he might have gone back out there." Mr. Woodhollow shook his head.

"Looking back I had convinced myself it was a bear, and it probably was. But I never disobeyed my daddy again, even after he passed on. So Jerry, this might sound like a scary story, a tall tale warning to keep out, because I suppose it is. I had passed this on to my own son years ago, but he didn't come home from that war in Korea, so I'm passing it on to you. Don't go back there, and don't tell others about that place."

It was late when Jerry left, and the sun had almost set. He wondered how true that story was, but he didn't waste any time riding home.

Jerry continued to do yardwork for Mr. Woodhollow several years after he quit his paper route, though they never talked much about the woods again. It was right after Jerry graduated from high school that Mr. Woodhollow passed away; Jerry and his parents attended the funeral. A probate hearing revealed Mr. Woodhollow had left him something, something that was to remain unopened until after Jerry had received his college degree, which he was able to pay for himself, both from Mr. Woodhollow's recommendation to save half of his earnings and his own 'Rainy Day Fund' suggested by his father.

Four and a half years later, a newly graduated Jerry and his parents again met with the probate lawyer, where it was revealed that the majority of the Woodhollow land had been left to Jerry, with a portion to be sold off for taxes due. His family was quite taken aback, as was Jerry. He had grown a lot over the years at college, and thought back to delivering that first paper to what he initially regarded as a spooky old house. He hadn't been there since Mr. Woodhollow had died.

It was late June when Jerry drove by the Woodhollow house. It had been boarded up and left to the elements, and they had not been kind. The house was now his, and he began making mental notes of all the repair that was required, though he had no intention of staying there. He walked round the back of the house. The rest of the yard had practically turned to a wild field once more, save the path that led back to the woods.

Jerry walked that path as tall grasses brushed up against his legs, and he thought back to the walks and hikes he and Mr. Woodhollow had taken, and all that he had learned about the woods. It had even influenced some of his college coursework, learning about forest management and geology. Inevitably the tale of the fenced-in still and the preacher's curse entered his mind, and he chuckled, remembering the tale quite fondly as one of the more colorful moments with old Mr. Woodhollow.

With old and new eyes he observed the forest as he followed remnants of the old trails, switching to game trails and even making a few of his own as he surveyed the land, crossing creeks and mounting crests. And then in the distance, he saw it: a portion of the fence.

Planks were missing here and there, but the structure was clearly recognizable despite the undergrowth. Jerry approached and wondered what real reason Mr. Woodhollow's father had wanted him to keep away from the site. Perhaps he had killed the preacher and buried him there, or it was a private cemetery, or part of the cave had given way.

No longer was Jerry the boy who believed in tall tales, who was once afraid to even approach the Woodhollow house. No, Jerry was living in the present, where things were real, and everything was explainable. He climbed over the fence and made his way up the hill through the brush.

At the top of the hill was an exposed rock outcropping, and as he got closer, a natural cave opening was visible, the front strewn with a mound of debris. "So this was it?" Jerry thought to himself.

And then the mound shifted.

Jerry was transfixed as the jumble of ancient copper tubing, corroded metal bits, branches and animal bones were pushed up off the ground. Except there was nothing underneath pushing. The various elements in the mound convulsed, and ever so briefly, Jerry thought it was stretching? —but that was completely insane —when his brain told him to RUN.

He ran down the hill and almost tripped jumping over the fence. He felt every nerve fire inside as adrenaline coursed through his body. Reason had been left behind, as Jerry was now completely operating on a fight or flight response, with fight being out of the question.

He could hear the thrashing of the cursed pile lurching down the hill, pursuing him, though he dare not look back. His heart felt like it would leap out of his chest, and it may have skipped a beat or stopped entirely when the thing behind him let out the most unearthly HOWL—SHRIEK.

Jerry sprinted and looked for a decent tree to climb, but was not veering much, only running AWAY from the threat, as he could hear it gaining on him as he crested a small hill and descended to the forest floor ahead —believing any second it would tear him to pieces. Then he smelled the stench —was it the foul thing's breath just over his shoulder?

He heard tree branches crash behind him, and placed the smell: skunk, or more likely skunk cabbage. Jerry bolted for the low-lying bog ahead where he knew the cabbage grew. He leaped as carefully as he could under the circumstances, zig-zagging to the clusters of grass and cabbage, the portions least likely to immediately sink when stepped on, and almost missed his last leap as he landed in a weak spot, where his shoe went under the muck.

He immediately wriggled his foot free, leaving the shoe behind and made a final few leaps across the bog as he heard the cursed debris pile catch up. He turned around to see the IMPOSSIBLE THING charge forward across the bog towards him, but the abomination quickly slowed as it was caught up, mired in the ooze.

It began to frantically thrash about as the mud slowly swallowed it up. It HOWLED one final time, and Jerry recoiled, thinking there was no possible way this could be real.

The muddy surface bubbled one last time and then was still. Jerry watched the surface of the bog long after the thing had sunk, well after any movement was detectable. The forest was quiet except for the pounding drum sound, which Jerry realized was his own heartbeat.

He took several deep breaths. Surely it had been a dream. A waking dream, he told himself over and over. Then he got up and walked out of the forest with his one remaining shoe.

It was a long time before Jerry returned to Woodhollow woods.

THE CAMPING TRIP

Craig, Jimmy, and Larry waited for Phillip. He was the last holdout, and was inside his house getting permission from his mom. Craig and Jimmy had already gotten the go-ahead from their parents, and Larry's parents were out of town, his older sister usually too occupied to notice his comings and goings.

Seated on the concrete porch, Larry fidgeted, and nibbled on his fingernails, Jimmy worked on his list of supplies they would need, and Craig stared at the clouds, his mind elsewhere. "Hey, what do you guys think of Jamie?"

Larry scrunched up his face and asked, "Jamie who?"

Without looking up from the list, Jimmy answered them both. "Jamie Calton. Craig's got a crush on her. But she's already going out with Donovan."

"Oh. Oh yeah. She's kind of funny. Too bad she's already got a boyfriend." Larry accentuated the word boyfriend.

Craig rolled his eyes. "He's a grade ahead."

Larry gave Craig an exaggerated dumbfounded expression. "It means he'll be out of middle school - he'll be at the high school this year," Craig explained.

"And she'll be lonely enough for the likes of you, eh Romeo?" Larry countered. Craig wound up to deliver a mock punch to Larry, who also put up his fists in a mock fashion.

"Out of sight, out of mind…good plan," Jimmy interjected, defusing the mock fight momentarily.

"Or absence makes the heart grow fonder," Jimmy added.

Craig kicked lazily at Jimmy, and Larry laughed. "Screw you both. Hey how long is —" The front door opened, and Phillip leaped out.

"I take it that's a yes?" Jimmy guessed.

"Yes! I got permission!" Phillip closed the door firmly behind him. "I kind of had to lie. I told my mom we're camping in Larry's backyard," Phillip confessed.

"Technically, we are," Jimmy corrected, and tore a page from his notepad, a checklist for each of them.

About an hour later they set off, laden with knapsacks and sleeping bags, down Larry's backyard and over the hill that led to acres of rolling countryside, old farmland that had been left to return to nature. Maple, hickory, and birch trees dotted the fields, and the boys made their way to the denser forest ahead, a part of a state preserve rarely traveled. Parking and the park entrance were miles away, and trails had yet to run to all portions. As a result, the back end of the preserve saw few casual visitors, and to the boys, represented untamed wilderness.

"Where are we headed?" Jimmy inquired as they entered the shade of the forest canopy.

"A cool place I found last week, an ideal spot for a campsite," Larry responded, while slashing at passing brush with a bowie knife.

"Don't cut yourself, Sinbad," joked Craig, and Phillip and Jimmy chuckled.

They hiked on for another half hour, and after cresting the final ridge emerged from the woods to enter a small circular clearing. Several medium sized aspen trees ringed the glade, and a massive oak stood at the edge near where they entered. "This is it." Larry held out his arms.

"Nice job Larry," congratulated Craig, as they surveyed their surroundings. A breeze blew across the brush, and the aspens rustled in accord.

They dropped their packs and decided on a place for the tent that Larry had brought. Jimmy thought it should be in the center of the clearing, but was out-voted for the flatter grass-free region under the big oak. Phillip began sweeping leaves from the spot with his foot, as Larry began unfolding the canvas tarp surrounding the rolled up tent.

"What are you doing?" Jimmy asked Phillip.

"Clearing out the crud… all the bugs and stuff," Phillip answered.

"Those leaves are going to keep the ground comfortable while you sleep," Jimmy explained. He had briefly been a boy scout, but his parents had withdrawn him after their divorce. He'd never actually been camping, but had read enough of his handbook.

"Well, pick a corner for your leaves, ya Webelo," Larry yelled, as he and Craig pulled the tarp out like a sheet. Jimmy pushed some of the leaves to one section, and Larry and Craig set the tarp over the ground. After several attempts and discussions on proper peg placement, the group had managed to finally erect the tent, in time for the onset of twilight.

Craig and Larry set out to gather firewood, and Jimmy insisted on fetching rocks to surround the fire, as his scout manual had suggested. Phillip stared across the clearing, noticing a lone deer on the far side watching them. He watched it long enough to wonder if it was real, until it finally flicked it's ears, and he turned briefly to tell the others, though after glancing back it had disappeared into the treeline.

Larry had brought along a pruning saw and began sawing at one of the oak's lower branches, while Craig collected fallen kindling dotting the area. Soon Craig had collected an armful of wood just as Larry finished sawing through his branch.

"There's plenty on the ground Larry, ya don't have to kill the tree," Craig remarked. Larry wiped the sweat from his brow with his shirt sleeve, and ignored his critic.

Jimmy had enlisted Phillip in lugging back the scattering of small rock boulders from the clearing, some pried from the ground with an old surplus shovel Jimmy had brought, and they soon had a circular fire pit lined with angled rock. Craig tossed his armful of firewood into the pit, and he began trying to light the mass with a lighter. After several failed attempts, Jimmy had produced his scout manual and began reading.

"It says you need some light kindling first, like some bark or dry grass," Jimmy related.

"It does? Let me see," Craig replied. Larry handed him the book, which Craig feigned interest in, before tearing out several pages of the book and tossing it back.

"Hey!" Jimmy scooped up his book. Craig lit the now crumpled papers and set them under the tinder, where the flame seemed to catch.

"I guess you were right." Craig smirked.

An exhausted Larry came back with one section of freshly cut branch about a foot long and set it near the fire pit. "Where's the rest of it?" Craig asked.

"I'm tired of sawing… I'll get some more in a bit." Larry reached for his pack, pulled out a metal canteen and drank several gulps of water.

"You better hurry, the sun's about to set," said Jimmy, who sprayed a can of insect repellent about.

Within the hour the sun had set, and the four were seated around the campfire, dining on blistered hot dogs, charred marshmallows, and drinking cans of soda. The fire cast light up the underside of the old oak and spilled out into the clearing.

When the flames began to diminish, Larry put his fresh cut branches on the fire, but after several minutes they only seemed to vent clouds of steam and white smoke rather than ignite.

After Phillip attempted to tell a story about a haunted blanket, Craig recounted a horror movie he had seen at the drive-in with his older brother, a real blood and guts extravaganza his parents wouldn't have let him see had they known. Larry told a story about the time his sister had used a Ouija board and got freaked out.

"Do you guys believe in ghosts?" Phillip asked. Craig scoffed at the idea.

Larry agreed, but Jimmy shook his head. "I don't know, you never know… like UFO's and Loch Ness. I saw this one show —"

"Or like Bigfoot!" Larry interrupted, which they all seemed to agree on, then realized they were in the woods at night. They glanced around, scanning the edge of the fire's glow.

Distant flashes snapped them out of their unease, as they spotted additional lightning flashes.

"Say Larry, is the tent waterproof?" Jimmy asked.

"Why sure... I think so," he answered. Several more flashes lit up the sky, eliciting some 'oohs' and 'aahs'.

"Think we should go?" Phillip wondered. Another flash.

"See that? Listen..." Craig said. They all listened over the crackle of the fire, crickets chirping, and the light rustle of the aspens.

"Nothing. It's probably just heat lightning, otherwise we should hear some thunder by now," Craig reasoned.

"Or else it's just really far away," Jimmy offered.

Before too long the light show subsided, the worry of rain passed. They continued talking until the fire began to wind down, the damp chill of the night began to set in, and they began getting ready to turn in.

"I gotta take a leak!" Jimmy said, before the rest followed suit, scattering around the immediate vicinity. Craig got some laughs when he started urinating on the fire, before walking to the grass beyond.

Within minutes they were in the tent, front flap zipped shut, and settled in their sleeping bags. Jimmy had a flashlight, and Phillip had a smaller penlight. Mention was made of the tent having a funky smell, which quickly gave way to simulated farting sounds from the group, before Larry let a real one rip, which filled the tent with laughter.

Not long after Jimmy turned out his light, Phillip followed suit, and chatter became sparse as each fell asleep.

Phillip woke first. The ground was no substitute for his bed, and he now wished he had covered the ground underneath with leaves like Jimmy had. He shifted over slightly, and turned onto his side, trying to get comfortable. Still he felt lumps, rocks or roots underneath. He shifted position again, and began to nod off.

"Hey cut it out. Quit poking me!" Craig broke the stillness. Phillip snapped awake.

"What? I didn't do anything," a groggy Larry reported.

"What are you guys going on about?" Jimmy asked, wiping his eyes in the darkness. Phillip turned on his penlight.

"Well someone keeps poking me," Craig complained.

"M-Me too!" added Phillip.

"It's just the roots in the ground. Go back to sleep," Larry grumbled, and then turned over inside his sleeping bag.

A moment later he sat up and said, "Alright, who's the wise guy?" Phillip shined the light over at Larry, and then around the tent.

"N-Nobody touched you Larry. I was watching," Phillip reported nervously. All four now sat up, peering around the tent.

"What about you Jimmy, you feel anything?" Craig asked.

"Nope, I told you guys you should have laid down some leaves, and you wouldn't be complaining like a bunch of —HEY! Something poked me!" Jimmy exclaimed.

"Really? W-What is it?" Phillip began to panic. "W-What if it's like b-bugs, or rats or something?" He frantically shone the light on each of their faces, then at the tent floor. "M-Maybe we ought to get out of here!" Jimmy switched on his flashlight, further illuminating the tent interior.

"Quiet! Listen!" whispered Craig. The two flashlights shone over at Craig's face, and he squinted disapprovingly, then motioned to turn them off. Jimmy turned off the larger flashlight, and Phillip tucked his inside his sleeping bag. The four craned their heads in the dark tent, trying to hear.

"What? Do you hear something out there?" Larry whispered back.

"I don't hear anything, Craig," Jimmy answered in a hushed voice. "That's just it - the crickets have stopped. It's way... too... quiet."

Slowly they all noticed the sound of a distant breeze, their tent still, the wind sound gaining in strength until—

...Instantly their shelter was buffeted by huge gusts of wind, the sides violently whipping about, the sound a roar. Moments later the wind abruptly ceased and calm returned, except for Phillip's screams. When he stopped, silence returned, except for their breathing.

"Was that a tornado?" Larry whispered.

"Jimmy, what was that?" asked Craig.

"I don't know… but… I think I just got poked again." Jimmy said.

"I know I just got p-poked again—I'm g-getting out of here!" Phillip jumped out of his sleeping bag, penlight in hand, scrambled over to the zipper and spilled out of the tent.

"Phillip don't go out there!" Jimmy warned, but the open flaps just dangled, and they heard Phillip's footfalls fade away from the tent into the woods towards home.

Jimmy switched his light back on, and the three looked at each other with wide eyes, unsure of what to do next. First they heard Phillip screaming nearby, then from above in the trees, and finally to fading shrieks more distant.

Only then did Craig frantically reach over and quickly zip the tent shut.

Then Jimmy's light went out. The three petrified boys suddenly knew they were not alone, that something —that MANY LARGE THINGS— were outside of their tent. Mortified, they hunkered as low to the ground as possible, in spite of the continued poking from below.

The night only got worse from there.

After wandering hysterically through the woods and briefly collapsing under a tree, the eventual light of dawn helped an exhausted Phillip make it home. His parents contacted the police. With the help of Phillip's description and a park ranger, the police were able to locate the boys campsite.

Once there they pulled three catatonic boys from a tattered but still-standing tent.

Only after several months of convalescing and psychiatric therapy were Craig, Larry and Jimmy able to regain their wits and function somewhat normally once more, though none of them would ever speak of what happened that night after Phillip ran off.

When Phillip's dad later accompanied the park ranger to collect the children's campsite belongings, the ranger realized where they had camped:

An undocumented and nearly forgotten historical site, of some of the earliest pioneers in the area. The stories told of an ancient homesteader colony from the late 1700's that had all died one year, their graves marked only by the stones that now lined the boys makeshift fire pit.

Later, Phillip's father dismantled the tent and removed the tarp, revealing a scattering of dirty white objects strewn about the loose soil.

Human finger bones. Of these, he did not tell Phillip.

JOHNNY'S SHORTCUT

Tracey stared out the window at tiny raindrops hitting the glass. She wondered if it would still be sprinkling, or even raining when it came time to walk home. That was still a few hours away, after her classes were to end, when she would find her younger brother and they would then walk the route back to their house.

Today they were going to stay a little longer, with permission from their mother to stay extra for the bookmobile that was visiting. Tracey had already read most of the interesting books in her school's meager library, and was excited to see what new offerings would be presented with this most recent visit. She was hoping for a good mystery.

Johnny, her younger brother, would probably want something with monsters, but not too scary. He really liked the creature pictures, but only if they were cartoony. Tracey would often read to him even though he was starting to learn to read on his own, though he still needed help with the big words.

Johnny always got excited when she was about to read him a story, and she enjoyed it as well. She remembered when he was still crawling around on all fours, and remembered her mom reacting to his first steps, even his first laugh. Though that was a long time ago, she made him laugh often and still thought he was adorable, kind of like a puppy that just kept getting smarter.

When class was over she put on her coat and hat and collected her book bag, then went to the front of the school with the rest of the departing children to look for Johnny. Most of the kids headed straight for the buses, but a few like herself were also headed to the bookmobile.

As she passed by the second set of gymnasium doors, she saw Johnny waiting. He was concentrating on a wooden puzzle maze game, and didn't notice Tracey approaching. "Hi Johnny, whatcha up to?" Tracey asked.

"Tryin' ta get the ball in the thingy…" Johnny replied.

"Where'd ya get that from?" Tracey asked.

"I found it in the trash can," said Johnny matter-of-factly.

"You shouldn't take things out of the trash, it might have germs," Tracey said.

"What are germs?" Johnny looked up at his sister.

"Bugs that can make you sick and barf," Tracey emphasized the word 'barf'.

"Ewww. It looked clean when the teacher threw it away. There was a new kid playing with it, and the teacher took it and threw it in the trash." Johnny held the puzzle at arm's length and continued, "I was going to give it back after class, but he was gone."

"Alright Johnny, in that case, you did a good thing." Tracey shifted her book bag.

"I did?" Johnny looked up surprised.

"Yep. Now are you ready to go check out all the cool books?" she teased. He nodded with a grin and threw the puzzle into his bag.

Tracey and Johnny made their way out to the parking lot where the large white book mobile was parked, and they stepped up the stairs on the converted delivery van. The inside was lined with shelves and racks, with sections displaying the various offerings. Tracey found a few potential candidate books, one involving an escaped horse, another of a girl who could talk to owls and learned to fly, and one of twin sisters who run away during the great depression. She chose the one with owls, her favorite bird.

Though she had already decided which book to purchase, she didn't want to rush her brother. With one eye on Johnny's browsing, she flipped through a magazine about bananas, or so she thought, finding it instead filled with pictures of actors and musicians.

Johnny was looking at the batch of picture books displayed, featuring everything from dragons, cowboys, and pirates. He marveled at the various adventures depicted, and focused in on several dinosaur books, though he already had several similar books at home. He noticed Tracey nearby and knew she was waiting, so he decided on a pop-up book about a lonely monster and showed it to her.

"Excellent choice my good man!" she complimented in a mock English accent she'd seen in a movie. She used this voice with Johnny when they played, and it always made him laugh, with no exception this time. Johnny emptied out his rubber coin holder. Tracey handed him a few dollar bills, letting him pay for their books.

The threat of rain long since subsided, they set out for the rear of the school to the playground, beyond which were rolling green fields and forests beyond. The larger forests were further away, and they would only pass by smaller glens along the path ahead. As they set forth along the trail, the hills undulated in such a way that soon the school behind them was no longer visible, only the trail ahead and behind could be seen. The effect was of being in a large bowl, nicknamed the 'punchbowl'. Around them swayed tall grasses, thick and some higher than Johnny was tall.

"Hey Tracey!" came a girl's shout from behind them. Tracey and Johnny turned around to see two girls, Trina and Andrea, following them up the trail. They paused until the girls caught up to them. "Are you just now getting home from school?" Andrea asked.

"Yeah, we stayed for the bookmobile, "Tracey replied.

"Oh was that today? Say did you see the new kid, Nicky?" asked Trina, wide-eyed.

Johnny knew he wasn't going to be a part of this conversation and looked around. They were in the center of the 'punchbowl', an area he remembered from the summer, having played here with his sister and some of the neighborhood kids. He stepped from the trail into the thick grass. He remembered a dugout hole in the ground close by that the other kids called the 'foxhole', and approached, wondering if it was still there. It was easier to spot in the summer when the grass was shorter; when they'd had what his father had called a drought.

Tracey listened to Trina talk about how she and Andrea were going to listen to a new record. They were in the process of inviting her, when she looked around to where Johnny had wandered into the grass. He had been in her periphery a moment ago, but was now out of sight. "Johnny?" She called out, stepping from the girls and the trail.

"Alright well, we gotta go, we'll see you later Tracey?..." She heard them, but her focus was now on finding Johnny, who was either playing hide and seek or exploring, hopefully not too far. She pushed further into the grass and weeds, following what look like the disturbed and broken grass trail of her brother.

She called out again "Johnny! Where are you?!" She started to grow concerned, and guilty for having been distracted by Trina and Andrea. She knew he was her responsibility, and didn't like the thought of Johnny getting lost… or certainly not being around. She didn't like that the last thought had entered her head, and yelled again: "Johnny can you hear me?"

"Here I am!" came the faint cry a few yards to her left. She couldn't see him but immediately turned to the sound of his voice, and charged through the grass, relieved to hear him.

A few steps further she called out "Where are you?" assuming he must be hiding in the thick growth, stopping to listen for his reply.

"Down here!" She took two steps forward and came to the edge of the foxhole. A few feet further and she would have fallen in, the one-by-two yard ellipse of the hole completely camouflaged by the overgrowth of grasses all around. Johnny stooped in the deeper portion of the hole, which was a little deeper than a yard. She remembered when they played here earlier in the year, Johnny had been reluctant to drop down into the hole, and though she had nearly stumbled in, was relieved to see that Johnny hadn't fallen in and been injured either.

"What are you doing down there?" She asked.

"I found some neat rocks! Check 'em out!" He held out his hand and she saw about a half dozen flecked quartz-like stones about the size of a large marble.

"That's great, but —" she said.

"And check this one out! It's the best one!" He held up a shiny black smooth stone larger than the rest.

"We ought be heading home Johnny. Mom isn't going to be too

happy about how dirty your shoes are."

"Oh yeah…" he agreed.

"Come on." She held out her hand to help him out of the hole. He stuffed the stones into his pockets and reached out to her hand. Tracey grabbed his hand, and when she began to pull, lost traction against the slick grass and slipped forward into the hole. They both screamed in surprise as she tumbled in, landing on her feet and butt, barely avoiding landing on Johnny.

"Rats," she said, dusting dirt off her pants as she stood in the hole.

"Rats? Where!" shouted Johnny.

"No silly, not REAL rats, I meant rats, mom is not going to be thrilled that we're both filthy," Tracey clarified.

"It's my fault… sorry," Johnny apologized.

She helped Johnny out of the hole first, then handed him his book bag. Hers had fallen off during the fall, and she knelt down to retrieve it and stuff back in the folders and new book that had partially fallen out. "Great—new book and already dirty," she thought to herself, and as she repacked her bag, she began to get an uneasy feeling.

Even though standing, her head above the edge of the foxhole, she suddenly didn't like being down in the hole alone. It must have been the tall grass surrounding, or perhaps a passing cloud, but it was not a place she wanted to remain much longer. Grabbing handfuls of grass close to the roots, she pulled herself up out of the hole.

She paused to look back in the foxhole, which once more seemed like the hole they had played in over summer. The clouds giving way to sun dispelled her thoughts, and she ushered them back towards the trail home once again.

The next morning Tracey and Johnny sat at the kitchen table eating french toast their mother had prepared, and Tracey noticed Johnny was particularly quiet this morning. "Hey—cat got your tongue?" Tracey teased.

"Huh? Oh. I had a weird dream last night... about the stones," Johnny answered.

"The ones from the foxhole? What was it about?" Tracey asked in between bites of toast.

"Well... I think... it's kind of a secret," Johnny reluctantly admitted.

Their mother came back into the kitchen to remind of the time, that they would be late for the bus as she could hear it approaching on an adjacent street. As they put on their shoes and gathered their knapsacks, their mother handed them paper sack lunches. "Can we walk home from school again Mom?" Johnny asked. Tracey rolled her eyes thinking he wanted to go look for more stones.

"Ok, but promise not to get dirty like yesterday, which goes for you too Tracey," said their mom. Tracey huffed in protest, but with the bus approaching, they quickly departed.

Only later in class did Tracey remember she'd forgotten to ask Johnny about his 'secret' dream. She'd told him some of the dreams she'd had in the past, though he struggled to remember his. She knew when he was making up his dream recollections, but she'd always humor him and listen anyway. Maybe he remembered a real dream. Keeping it secret seemed odd though, as he was always eager to share, at least try to keep up with Tracey's tales.

When school had ended and she walked to meet Johnny by the gym, she observed him handing the wooden puzzle game to a slight boy with blonde hair. "Did you finish it?" asked the blonde kid.

"Yep, it was easy," Johnny smiled. The blonde haired boy thanked him and ran off as Tracey approached.

"Soooo we're walking home again, no buses?" Tracey asked.

"Nope. no buses. I wanted to race home." Johnny explained.

"You mean hurry, or race me?" Tracey asked.

"I want to race you! If I win you clean out the kitty litter... the rest of this week!" Johnny said. His challenge was endearing, and as always, she played along.

"Alright well, if I win, what do I get?" Tracey asked.

Johnny thought briefly. "If you win, you can have my Hawaii coin."

She knew he was serious about this wager; he treasured the Hawaiian coin their grandmother had given him. "That's seems a pretty steep bet Johnny. How about if I win YOU do the cat litter the rest of the week. I'll even give you a head start," Tracey counter offered.

"Hmmmn. Ok... but wait here," he requested. They stopped at the corner of the school building, around which was the rear yard to the field-trail home.

"Alright, I'll count to ten. But get ready to scoop some kitty poop! Go!" Tracey shouted. Johnny ran around the corner towards the trail; while Tracey knelt down to tie her shoes, as she knew she might need to do a little bit of running to catch up, to at least make the race a challenge for him. She finished calling out her count, expecting to see Johnny still in the schoolyard, running for the trailhead. "Eight. Nine. Ten!" She turned the corner.

But Johnny was nowhere to be seen. Maybe he'd gotten faster than she remembered? She began running towards the trail entrance, again expecting to pick up sight of him further down the trail. Still no sight of Johnny. He must have sprinted, so surely once the trail veered left and went uphill into the rolling fields he would have run out of steam and she would catch up, she reassured herself. She sprinted past where the conversation with Andrea and Trina had taken place yesterday, and kept telling herself he must be just over the next hill, obscured by the tall grass and curves in the trail.

Only as she was nearing their house did she have the feeling that maybe something had happened to him along the way. Perhaps he had veered from the trail and tried to cut through the field... Or what if he had fallen into the foxhole again, or some other hole in the field? As doubts began to accumulate she was nearly at the house, and before panicking further, decided she should at least check the house first.

Tracey got to the side door and unlocked it with her key, then let the door slam shut behind her. She ran inside without taking off her shoes, which tracked in a little leftover dirt. "Mom! mom! Is Johnny here? mom!?" She yelled, running into the kitchen.

"Tracey!? Why are you shouting?" Her mother stood by the sink with a sponge in hand, the faucet running.

Johnny sat at the kitchen table, eating celery sticks filled with peanut butter. He grinned innocently at Tracey between crunching on stalks.

Tracey gaped at her brother. "Mom, when did Johnny get home?"

Her mother answered. "Oh several minutes... Tracey! You tracked dirt in, and I just mopped the floor. Go take off your shoes and get the broom. You know better than that. I shouldn't have to keep cleaning up after you two." Their mother sighed. Johnny looked down as Tracey walked back to the utility room.

After dinner Tracey finished cleaning out the cat litter box, then popped her head into Johnny's room. He was lying on his bed with the pop-up book, moving a lever to make a cutout monster's claw wave goodbye. "Alright, so how'd you do it. What route did you take, and if you don't fess up, the tickle monster is gonna have to pay a visit, a visit… when you least expect it!" Tracey held up a menacing hand, her fingers splayed. Johnny was familiar with the tickle monster, and they both knew he was powerless against it.

"OK, OK, no tickle monster! I surrender! Uncle!" he yelped as Tracey loomed with both hands outstretched.

"It was the rocks and the dream! It showed me," Johnny confessed.

"Rocks? You mean the rocks from the foxhole yesterday?" Tracey asked, and Johnny nodded. "And the dream from last night, the secret you couldn't tell me this morning?" she continued. Again Johnny nodded sheepishly. Tracey lowered her tickle monster hands and sat down onto Johnny's bed. Johnny, relieved from the tickling threat, crossed his legs scooting to lean against the headboard.

"Well, I wanted to tell you, but I wasn't supposed to," Johnny said.

"Says who?" Tracey asked.

"In my dream, it was supposed to be a secret, but I don't know who said it. It wasn't words. I just knew." Johnny scrunched up his face, trying to further articulate his thoughts.

"I… I think it was the rocks. They told me to make the circle, but carry the black one with me, and to keep it a secret," he said.

"Time for bed you two," interrupted their mother, standing at the threshold of Johnny's doorway. After a minor appeal to stay up later that was denied, Tracey got up from the bed and headed off to her room. Getting into bed, she fell asleep with more questions than answers.

That night she dreamt of swimming in a huge black ocean, vast and deeper than measure, and when her mother finally woke her, she'd had to scramble to get ready, having slept through her own alarm. She and Johnny barely made the bus, and the remnants of the dream clung like fog in her head.

By lunch she'd fully awoken, and would have quizzed Johnny further had they shared lunch time, but the younger grades ate at the cafeteria first. He had to be making something up, had to be playing a trick on her. No matter, she decided, they'd just have to race again today. And this time, no head start.

After school Tracey and Johnny walked to the backside of the school, to the rear yard that led to the field and trail home. "Ok, so what's the secret? We can race again, but I won't make any bets until you spill the beans." Tracey raised an eyebrow at Johnny. He fished his hand in his pocket, and pulled out the shiny black rock, and handed it to her.

In her hands it was polished smooth, but had a few subtle facets that weren't immediately noticeable. "If I hold this rock, it will take me back to the other rocks. Yesterday and today I put them in a circle in my room before school, like in my dream." Johnny said.. She handed it back to Johnny.

"And you went from here... to your room?" She regarded him with skepticism. "Prove it."

Johnny looked around the schoolyard and furrowed his brow. There was no one else around. "Well, you have to look away," Johnny requested.

"What? Why?" Tracey asked.

"For it to work, no one can see. That's the secret," Johnny answered. Tracey stared at him, waiting for him to drop the act, but he was as serious as she'd seen him. Exasperated, she threw up her hands.

"Fine." Tracey turned away from him. "For how long?" She snuck a peek over her shoulder.

Johnny was gone. There was nowhere he could have run in the two seconds her eyes were averted. "There is no way", she thought. "No way at all." She collected her wits and began running to the trail surrounded by the ocean of grass. Halfway along the trail Andrea and Trina called out to her from nearby, though she doubted they heard her apologies for not stopping. She sprinted up over the hill into the punchbowl, past the foxhole, and slowed as she struggled to catch her breath.

Once her house was nearly in sight, she gained a second wind, and ran through the remaining field and treeline up into the backyard. She ran to the side door and fumbled for the key in her pockets, but realized that in her haze this morning she'd forgotten it. Tracey ran around to the front door, nearly slipping in the gravel driveway as she turned the corner, and rang the doorbell repeatedly.

From the front porch she could hear the vacuum cleaner turn off. Her mother opened the front door. "Tracey, what —" Tracey rushed in past her. "Young lady, shoes!" her mother admonished. Tracey ran down the hall, poking her head into each bedroom and bathroom, excitedly opening each door.

"Mom! Is Johnny here?" she yelled from the back of the house. "Have you seen Johnny yet?" She ran into Johnny's room. Like the rest of the house, the room was completely tidied up, the carpet vacuumed—

And not a trace of the rock circle.

"Mom!?" yelled Tracey.

Her mother stood at the doorway. "He should be with you. You didn't leave him behind—" She cocked her head in concern. "Did you two race again?" her mother asked.

"Mom, what did ...were there ...did you see any rocks in here?" Tracey shouted at her mother, who shot her a stern look. "I'm sorry Mom, yeah... we were racing —but please, were there some rocks in here today?"

"Well yes, but I tossed them out into the driveway with the rest of the rocks."

Tracey's face went ashen.

She bolted from the room and past her mother once more, down the hall and living room to the front door. "Tracey!" her mother yelled. Tracey threw open the front door and leaped out to the porch. The driveway was filled with thousands, perhaps tens of thousands of small rounded chunks of grey-white limestone. Somewhere among them were the white flecked quartz stones that had made up the circle, indistinguishable from the limestone.

Tracey kneeled down over the gravel, panic in her heart and tears welling up in her eyes. "If I can just make the circle, Johnny won't be lost," she thought, and began to sob, tears streaming down her cheeks as she frantically poked and scanned over the countless rocks.

Dark spots. She saw dark spots on the limestone gravel, and quickly realized they were from her tears. Tracey remembered when it rains the driveway gravel goes dark. As her mother came to the front door, Tracey darted around the corner to the side yard, where a coil of garden hose hung from the side of the house. She spun the wheel of the attached faucet, and freed the hose from the hanging mount.

Water pouring from the end, Tracey ran with the available hose around the corner to the front of the house, but nearly lost her footing as the hose ran out several yards from the driveway. "Tracey, what are you doing?" her mother called out, now from the front window, though Tracey ignored her. She pressed her thumb tight against the open end of the hose, creating pressure and causing it to spray, and spray she did, thoroughly showering and wetting down the driveway gravel nearest the house. Saturated, the limestone went dark.

There was the first!

She spotted the flecked quartz marble stone, shining and contrasting from the surrounding dark limestone. She threw down the gurgling hose, and within a minute she had scooped up several, hoping she had found them all, with no more immediately visible. She opened the front door again, this time sloshing wet footprints all the way back to Johnny's room. "Tracey!" she heard her mother exclaim from the kitchen.

She laid out the flecked quartz stones in a large circle on the floor, about a yard in diameter. She heard her mother coming down the hall. "YOUNG LADY!" she shouted from the doorway, and Tracey turned to see her mother's fury...

"Oh—you're home. Tracey! Clean up this mess and for the LAST time, take off your shoes!" Her mother turned and walked away.

"Hey, how did you beat me?" Johnny asked, and Tracey spun around to see him standing in the center of the stone circle, just as she'd seen him at the schoolyard. She lunged forward and hugged him tightly in relief, fresh tears streaming down her cheeks.

After dinner, Tracey quietly slipped into the garage and retrieved a shovel. She took all the stones and stuffed them into a paper lunch bag and snuck outside. Far out in the field beyond her backyard, Tracey dug as deep of a hole possible before the sun set, and she buried the bag of stones, filling and hiding evidence of the hole before returning home.

She'd buried the stones deep. Just like the previous owners had.

SEPTEMBER RAINBOW

"Hey Mike, did your mom make any of that dip like last time?" Eric called from the kitchen. In the dining room Mike was explaining the rules again to Evan.

His character had been killed in a fantasy board game, having first been knocked unconscious and then slowly dying before anyone could stop his character's bleeding.

Will came down the stairs from using the bathroom, and could see Evan's frustration. "Sorry Evan, but we were tied up fighting those goblins," He offered. Eric called out from the kitchen about the dip again.

Evan protested. "I don't see why one of you couldn't—"

Eric came into the dining room after slapping the back of Evan's head. "Give it a rest. You were sneaking around too much. You got killed. Mike—any of that dip?"

Mike was about to answer when Evan flipped the books in front of him and stood up to face Eric. "Screw you and the stupid dip! I'm tired of you picking on me! And to hell with this game!" Evan grabbed his coat, stormed off and headed downstairs to the back door for his shoes.

Will and Mike exchanged wide-eyed expressions, somewhat familiar with Evan's tendency to get hot under the collar. "You probably shouldn't have hit him," Mike offered.

"It was just a smack," Eric shrugged.

"Is he leaving?" Will asked.

"Don't think so. I drove, and its nine miles back to his house," Eric explained. They heard the back door open and slam shut.

"Maybe he is leaving," Will concluded.

"Well, I think his bike is still here from last time," Mike mentioned.

"Well, he kind of brought this on himself, sneaking around, pick pocketing, and then attempting to backstab the goblin lord before the rest of us could catch up. And don't get me started on that blowgun of his. Couldn't hit the side of a barn," Eric complained.

Earlier Evan had brought along a homemade blowgun to show off, similar to the one his in-game character carried. A demonstration showed he clearly needed more practice.

Will collected his dice and placed them into a suede pouch. "Are we still playing?" It was relatively early on that autumn night, considering they'd gotten a late start with the game.

Everyone's schedules were becoming harder and harder to coordinate, with some of them recently licensed to drive, a few with jobs, and even a possible girlfriend for Will on the horizon. As it was they were playing without one of their usual group; Frank had been forced to fill in at the pizza parlor for a no-show.

For the last few years they had gathered here at Mike's house on the occasional Saturday, playing until well past midnight, when Mike's mom would usually shoo them for the night. But this weekend Mike's parents were away, and they decided to go ahead and play without Frank present, with Mike temporarily controlling his character.

Illuminated by the single streetlight visible outside the dining room window, the wind blew through the tall maple and oak trees, dislodging countless leaves. The headlights of a distant car shone on the trees and danced across the branches as it pulled into the driveway of Mike's house.

"Is your Mom home early?" asked Eric. The doorbell rang. Mike got up from the kitchen table and answered the door.

"Hey—am I too late?" Frank stood at the front door with a pizza box and his backpack in hand. Mike motioned for Frank to come in, but reminded him about taking off his shoes.

"I'd say you're right on time," Eric took the pizza box and backpack from Frank.

"I've actually got some more pizzas downstairs, but I wasn't sure if we were still on, I mean I saw Evan leaving on his bike," Frank pointed up the street.

"Yeah, he got killed, and he's kind of… upset," Will admitted.

Eric had set the pizza box down on the kitchen table and opened it with sudden disappointment. "All pepperoni?" He complained. Frank motioned back downstairs while Mike let him out to retrieve the additional pizzas.

Will helped himself to a slice of pizza and asked no one in particular, "Think he'll come back?" Eric glanced from the pizza to Will, almost registering a hint of remorse for escalating things, when Frank returned with the additional pizza boxes.

Mike handed out plates as they sat around the table, and Eric opened the next box. "There's a few slices missing — you get hungry on the way over Frank?" Eric inquired.

"Huh? Oh, I just had them grab whatever leftovers were around," Frank replied and grabbed a slice from the second box after Eric removed several pieces.

Multiple slices of pizza later, washed down by numerous cans of an off-brand cola Mike's mom kept the house stocked with, the group debated whether to continue playing for the night. Evan's departure had kind of taken the steam out of the evening and they began to stray off topic. The possibility of renting some zombie movies or checking what was on cable was floated, though Mike informed them that his Mom had switched from Cinemax to HBO, which made them all groan.

Frank lit up. "That's right, I almost forgot. You all know Mr. Pfarner, the shop teacher from middle school?" He asked.

"Yeah, that jerk gave me a D on my crossbow project," Eric sneered. Mike and Will also acknowledged, all of them having taken his shop class several years prior.

"Well he came in the shop earlier today and ordered some pizza while I was in the back. The owner was up front and I could hear them talking. I guess he lives too far for delivery according to the owner, way out in the unincorporated areas."

"The owner is always chatting everybody up and usually the rest of us are making fun of him, but it was just me in the back tonight on account of everyone else was out on delivery, so I got to 'eavesdrop' a little," Frank continued, having gotten the group's attention. "So he starts asking Mr. Pfarner about the old Starlight motel sign out that way."

"Oh the place that burned down years ago, just that sign still standing," said Will.

"Yep that's the one, the owner is asking about history of the motel. Mr Pfarner starts telling him about how it was opened in the fifties, then changed hands several times in the sixties until the commune bought it," Frank said.

"The what? Did you say commune — like communists?" Eric asked, cocking his head.

"No, more like hippies. It was some kind of hippie commune. Apparently a bunch of society dropouts moved in and took it over, and started attracting followers from the college and whereabouts and growing in numbers. When they got too big to house everyone, they built a bunch of buildings deeper in the woods behind the motel," Frank explained.

"How far back are we talkin'? We've all gone past that thing plenty of times and not seen any buildings. Did those burn down too?" Will asked.

"Real far back, according to Mr. Pfarner. They wanted to get away from society, you know, drop out. They even tried to set up a farm and have animals. That's when they abandoned the motel. They used to come into town occasionally, really stood out from the locals, were the talk of the town for awhile. I guess there was a lot of fear some of the local kids might be tempted to join, but apparently our town was a little too square for any of that to happen," Frank paused to finish his soda.

"So there was a lot going on back then apparently, and nobody really noticed when they stopped coming around. Maybe around '72 or '73 Mr. Pfarner guesses. Apparently someone went out to check on them eventually, and found the place deserted. A mess, but abandoned. A bunch of buildings over an acre, with a big building in the center that must have been their meeting hall." Frank said.

"So what happened?" Mike asked.

"Nobody knows what happened to the commune, but apparently, about a mile in the woods from the sign, it's all still there," Frank whispered.

They all glanced at each other; unaware to the extent they were absorbed in the story, until Eric broke the silence. "We should go there. Tonight!"

"Well, that doesn't seem like a bad idea. Oh wait. That is a bad idea. I've seen way too many horror movies," Will quipped.

Eric went to the fridge and popped the top of a can of beer. Mike was about to protest, as Eric took a gulp and tried to hide his displeasure at the taste. "Oh come one! It'll be an expedition. We'll bring some weapons for just in case. It'll be a real-world adventure. What do you say Frank?" Eric passed the beer to Frank, putting him on the spot, who glanced over to Will and Mike.

"I can't believe we've never heard of it. I thought we knew everything about this area," Mike muttered to himself.

"Come on, what else are we going to do tonight, sit around watching movies? There'll be four of us, and this is an opportunity to not be a bunch of nerds sitting around playing a game, but to be… adventurers!" Eric coaxed the group.

Glances were exchanged as each of them considered Eric's suggestion, who then tried a different approach. "Mike—think how much it could help with the realism—think of the role-playing!" He urged.

Mike raised an eyebrow, seeing the potential. "I do have that ceremonial sword my grandfather gave me…" He confirmed. "It's kind of small, isn't it? I'm calling dibs on your dad's machete in the garage," Eric insisted.

Frank took a gulp of the beer and then another. "What else have you got in the garage?"

Focusing on the final holdout, Eric began to recoil and pantomimed shaking his hands. "What do you say, Will? You're not... "Eric clutched his chest dramatically.

"Don't say it. I'm in," Will interrupted, shaking his head.

Within minutes they were perusing the hardware assortment in Mike's garage, arming themselves for battle with various tools and gardening implements. "Hey Mike, does your dad have any guns around? You know, just in case?" Will asked.

Eric interrupted, mimicking Mike's voice: "That wouldn't be authentic weaponry..."

Mike stared at Will briefly, then reached for a dirty plastic case from a top shelf. He blew off the dust and from within produced an orange plastic pistol. "Yeah, let's leave the toys behind," Eric chuckled.

"It's not a toy. It's a flare gun. My dad has had this up here ever since he sold the boat a few years ago. Probably forgot about it. This might qualify as a 'magic missile'," Mike smirked.

"Hey, you know what? That reminds me," Eric set down his new machete and went outside. Frank hefted a crowbar in one hand, a hatchet in the other. Eric burst back in and dramatically presented what he had been looking for. A wooden boomerang.

The group jeered at him. "Eric, were you ever able to get that thing to work?"

"Yeah—there was that one time I caught it," Eric insisted.

"After all the crap you gave Evan about the blowgun?" Mike

reminded.

"Hey, if you're bringing a magic missile, I'm bringing my trusty boomerang," Eric declared with extra flair.

"More like your 'trusty stick,'" Frank quipped, and the group chuckled.

After a discussion about redundant flashlights, they piled into Frank's car, armed and ready.

The ridiculousness of their endeavor began to set in as they drove on, and when Mike tried to narrate as if they were on a 'quest', the role-playing quickly dismantled into crude jokes about 'pillaging the townsfolk'. Mike knew it was hopeless and soon found himself laughing as well at their cavalier boasts.

Within twenty minutes they pulled off the road and onto the cracked asphalt of what remained of the Starlight motel. The rusty sign still had most of its letters, and traces of bird's nests remained from earlier in the season. Frank switched on the high beams as the car crept forward, transitioning from asphalt to gravel.

Along one side tall grass clusters and piles of leaves barely concealed remnants of the motel's foundation, while the other side was scattered with shrubs and thorny bushes. If the sign wasn't still visible, one would never notice this place from the road.

Frank weaved around a dense stand of underbrush, then slowed and parked before the gravel ran out. Will looked out the back towards the sign and saw they were far from sight of the road. The headlights shone into the woods beyond, revealing an overgrown dirt road beckoning.

Eric was the first out and switched on his flashlight, tucking his boomerang inside his rear belt, and then unsheathed the machete from the scabbard looped to his belt. Frank switched off the car as the rest of them got out. With the headlights off and far from the lights of their familiar neighborhoods, the darkness was at first overwhelming.

"Whose idea was this?" Will asked. They chuckled uneasily.

Mike switched on a lantern flashlight, the most powerful of their various light sources, and their eyes slowly adjusted to their surroundings. Soon the sky and stars helped to silhouette what remained of the leaves atop the trees surrounding them.

There was just enough chill in the air to make them glad they had worn fall coats, a few of them having borrowed extra sweatshirts from Mike's closet.

They followed the muddy road deep into the woods, and were soon far from the car. "Shouldn't this path be overgrown?" Mike wondered aloud.

"What the hell is that?" Eric swung his flashlight around to an incongruous shape surrounded by saplings and covered in vines. The rest of their lights quickly illuminated the rusting frame of an old oil well, long since seized up and abandoned.

"Cripes Eric, don't do that!" Mike let out a sigh.

"I might need to change my shorts!" Frank uneasily chuckled. Eric lowered his machete.

"Yeah, don't get all Don Kwix-o-tee on it," Will said.

They stared at the contraption for a few more moments before continuing deeper into the woods. "Actually it's pronounced Kee-yo-tee," Mike corrected.

"Whatever," Will mumbled.

"But Will makes a good point. "Frank, you didn't set us out on another snipe hunt, did you?" Mike asked.

"Hey guys, don't look at me, this was Eric's idea. I just told you what I overheard," Frank countered.

"Alright you guys, don't tell me you're getting... scared?" Eric challenged, which seemed to evoke some bluster from the group.

"We've made it this far," Mike said with a sigh, and they continued along the road.

The light breeze that had been creeping through the trees began to diminish as the group started to doubt their endeavor, until Mike's flashlight found something up ahead. "No way," he muttered.

Ivy vines could not obscure the first of the wooden shacks visible up ahead, and it was clear that time and the elements had not been kind to the structure. Cracked and peeling paint coated the walls, it's original color unknown, while the tar paper roof top sagged with sundry holes and water damage.

They peered in various windows to see unknown detritus, piles of leaves and rotting clothes, with walls covered in water stains, splotched with several colors of mold.

"Well Frank, This sure ain't no snipe hunt," Mike said.

"How far back do you think we are?" Will asked.

"It's got to be at least a mile, mile and a half," Frank guessed.

"I still can't believe this has been here all this time, and we'd never heard of it," Mike uttered.

Several more shacks were evident nearby, and their flashlights lit up the myriad of abandoned structures.

A few small trees and saplings intruded upon what were once walkways connecting the shacks, but the original layout was still evident. All of the buildings were roughly similar in size, each with metal frames for bunk beds visible through broken windows and open and hanging doors.

"Hey Mike, shine your light over here," Eric requested. Several buildings in they could see additional units scattered in both directions, but what caught their attention was the larger building in the center, a circular kiva-like structure roughly 50 feet in diameter.

This structure differed in that the windows had been completely boarded up, and appeared to have suffered less from the elements.

"What the hell? Do you think this was like—their meeting hall?" Will wondered.

"More like their church," Eric replied. They slowly circled the round hall surveying the surroundings, revealing nearly a dozen more similar shacks, and several rusted vehicles near the decaying remains of an ancient school bus. A light breeze blew through the area, and the surrounding treetops swayed in unison.

"We should check out each of these cabins. Let's split up," Eric suggested in a mock voice. Several curse words later they realized he was joking, being a horror movie cliché they had all discussed on more than one occasion. The joke did lighten the mood briefly.

"We came, and we found it. Um, shall we get going?" Mike suggested.

"Not until we have a look inside there," Eric motioned with his machete back towards the round building. "Any of you see a door?" He scrutinized the exterior, shining his light across planks and faded wooden siding.

"Hey Frank, come over here," Eric beckoned, and then traded his machete for the crowbar in Frank's hand. He pocketed his flashlight and set to work prying off several boards covering up a featureless door. Jamming the crowbar around the door's edge, he finally located a decent purchase, and attempted to force the door open.

His attempts less than persuasive being on the slender side, Frank tapped him on the shoulder and offered him back his machete. Frank was the largest of the group, something even Eric couldn't argue with. He took the machete and stepped aside.

KRee-ACK! With his full weight Frank forced the door open, and they all recoiled at the gust of putrid air coming from within. "Still want to go in there?" Will warned and waved his hands to dissipate the odor.

"What the hell is that, rotten eggs?" Mike gagged and spit on the ground.

"Dang! Someone needs to lighten up on the burritos," Frank wrinkled up his nose and then made a fart sound with his mouth. They copied the sound effect, laughing and defusing the apprehension. Eric shined his light in first, followed by the stronger beam of Mike's light. They peered through the doorway.

One by one they stepped over the threshold and into the circular hall. Cobwebs hung from the walls and ceilings, and they noticed first the concentric arrangements of homemade bench pews. Three rings worth of pews, each interior set lower than the previous. The effect was of a lowered circular stage, with seating for dozens.

Gradual sloping staircases made of similar wood interspersed the seating, and the stage had tiered steps encircling it. As they focused their lights upon the stage they could see a circular railing centered on the stage, the railing surrounding an opening about eight feet in diameter.

Emboldened by their discovery, they slowly stepped down towards the central stage, shining flashlights around the pews and floors. A few moldy papers and books were scattered about the hall, unidentifiable under layers of dust.

Eric was the first to approach and step up onto the stage, the timbers creaking beneath his feet as he neared the railing.

"Hey you guys, check this out. Hey Mike, bring that light over here," Eric beckoned. Mike and the others stepped up onto the stage and to the railing edge. They each shone their flashlights into the hole in front of them, but apart from the stage floor edging, the light was swallowed up and revealed nothing.

"What the hell is this?" Will gulped.

"What kind of church has a hole in the center?" Mike wondered. He kept his light directed towards the hole while the others shone elsewhere, re-illuminating the room faintly once more.

Eric stepped off and reached for a moldering book, kicking up a cloud of dust. Clusters danced in and out of their flashlight rays, particles undisturbed for years. He stepped back to the rail's edge and released the book from his grasp.

They all leaned in to listen, but no sound escaped the hole. "Ok, I think I've seen enough," Will declared and turned back to the doorway—and froze. "Uh, we've got a guest," He stammered.

The others spun around to see a tall figure silhouetted in the doorway. Their weaker lights shone on the visitor, and Frank breathed a sigh of relief tinged with surprise. "Oh, it's Mr. Pfarner."

Mike shone his light at the man, confirming his identity. "Sheesh Mr. Pfarner, you about gave us a heart attack," Mike took a few steps forward, then—

KK-KKEWWW! Mr. Pfarner fired a pistol at their feet, tiny splinters and dust shot up from the floorboard. Mike could feel the blood draining from his face. "Whoa, What the…" Eric took a step and—

KK-KKEWWW! Another bullet tore into the wood a few feet from Eric's shoe. "Put down the weapons, boys," Mr. Pfarner insisted. Mike and Will quickly complied, followed by Frank setting down his crowbar with Eric finally tossing his machete to the edge of the platform.

"Um, we're... sorry for trespassing Mr. Pfarner?" Frank stammered.

"Trespassing? Who else knows you're here?" Mr. Pfarner asked, as he stepped across the threshold, and slowly approached them.

"Uh, I told my mom. And my dad," Mike volunteered. Mr. Pfarner coolly gazed at Mike.

"You should never lie to a man with a gun," His gaze switched over to Frank. "You're not trespassing, Frank. You're my guest. I invited you with that story earlier tonight. I just didn't think you'd bring... all your friends," He added, stepping closer to the stage they stood upon.

"You 'invited' me?" Frank gulped. Eric glanced over at his machete. Mr. Pfarner saw this and raised his pistol in Eric's direction.

"I think I'd like all of you to step back, round the other side, away from your... weapons," He commanded. They grudgingly sulked around the opening to the far side of the hole. Mr. Pfarner slowly stepped up onto the stage.

"*You* killed the cult members," Eric accused. Mr. Pfarner squinted at him then let out a hearty chuckle that dully echoed throughout the hall.

"You've got me all wrong, son. I've never killed anyone. And I loved the people here. September Rainbow was our name. They were my family, my brothers and sisters, especially Barbara, the most beautiful girl you've ever seen.

"We all had a purpose and a role. Mine—was of a carpenter. I'd built most of what you've seen tonight. We'd made our own garden of Eden, surrounded by mother nature, with food provided by our crops and water from a spring, there," he pointed at the hole.

The boys shifted uneasily, blocked from the only exit by an armed hippie turned shop teacher who wanted to lecture them.

"It should have been left alone, but someone wanted to widen the spring opening. When they began digging, a small sinkhole formed, and the spring stopped. Everyone agreed that this was a sign. I went off to fetch more lumber for a platform around the hole, and when I returned, the hole was much, much, bigger. And they were all gone," Mr. Pfarner's voice trailed off.

"I didn't know what to do. I thought they'd all left and abandoned me. But then I heard a voice. It was... Barbara. From the hole. She promised to return, that they'd all return. But they were lonely, and couldn't return until... the loneliness was gone."

Eric and Will glanced at each other, while Mike and Frank seemed mesmerized by Mr. Pfarner's tale.

"Well, I've rambled on long enough. You boys must be sick of hearing me lecture," He casually remarked. They each seemed to relax at the shift in his tone.

"Into the hole with you," Mr. Pfarner aimed the pistol at Mike's head. Mike's jaw dropped, his mouth agape.

"You must be kidding, Mr. Pfarner right? This is a helluva joke, sir!" Eric stammered, incredulously. Mr. Pfarner redirected his aim to Eric's head.

"No joke son, all of you go in the hole, and Septem — Barbara, returns, comes back to me," he declared.

Suddenly Eric noticed a new shape at the building's entrance. PWITH! a sound issued from the figure. Mr. Pfarner lurched forward slightly, reaching one hand behind his neck as he slowly spun around. They could see an orange colored dart sticking out of Mr. Pfarner's back.

Mike directed his flashlight towards the shape and revealed Evan attempting to reload a fresh dart into his blowgun. KK-KKEWWW! Mr. Pfarner fired a shot at Evan, who fell back through the opening.

"Hey!" yelled Mike, and they began to scramble for cover as Mr. Pfarner swung his attention back to them, all except for Eric who had withdrawn the boomerang from his rear belt, took a deep breath, wound up and hurtled the curved piece of wood directly at Mr. Pfarner.

KRACK! The boomerang hit him squarely in the face, and he began to stumble, clearly disoriented. The boys ran around the stage to exit towards the hall's only door, and briefly turned back when they heard Mr. Pfarner's voice.

He tried to step after them, his face marked by a big red gash, but his equilibrium was not up to the task.

"Wait, come—Barbara..." He stepped forward first, then drunkenly lurched to the side, before overcompensating and finally pitching back towards the hole. The railing caught him briefly, before cracking and giving way. Pistol still in hand, Mr. Pfarner tumbled backwards into the void.

The hall fell silent, the group vaguely registering what had just transpired. Frank and Will were just outside picking up Evan, with Mike and Eric just inside the doorway keeping a wary eye on the hole. "Evan—is he?" Eric asked.

"I fell back when I saw that gun point at me. Otherwise, I'm fine," Evan stood up and brushed himself off.

"How did you know we were here?" Will inquired.

"And how did you get here?" Mike added.

"Well, I saw Frank drive up to your house earlier, and thought he might be bringing along some pizza. I was still pissed — I still am angry at you Eric, but after stealing a few slices of pizza from the car figured I'd hang around to prank you — try to scare you guys but good.

"But then I overheard Frank's story. Never thought you would come out here, but I figured it would be the perfect place to make you crap your pants. I took your bike, Mike, mine's not as fast. Hope you don't mind," He explained with a smirk.

"Don't mind at all. What took ya?" Mike said, his voice still shaking with adrenaline.

"You pedal four miles on a belly full of pizza. Thought I was gonna puke when I got here, positive I was going to blow the scare. Never counted on Mr. Pfarner. What a nut," Evan remarked.

"Certifiable," added Frank, and they all chuckled grimly.

Eric stepped towards Evan, and held out his hand. "Look, I was an ass; I do things I don't mean. I never meant anything by it, and— I'm sorry."

Evan glanced at Eric's outstretched hand, scrunched up his face and responded. "You're right. You are an ass. You've got a loud mouth. But if you didn't, I probably couldn't have snuck close enough—" Suddenly his eyes grew wide as his voice trailed off.

The others instantly picked up his body language, and Eric briefly though he was playing a trick, until Mike directed his beam back toward the stage and hole where a faint vapor could be seen rising from the hole.

Then came the SOUND.

A howling-moaning echoing from deep within the hole, spawning a primordial shiver that gripped their spines. All were transfixed as more gaseous mist rose up, the moaning from the hole rising nearer to the surface, the ground beginning to vibrate beneath their feet.

Mesmerized by the spectacle, they almost didn't smell the growing odor of something worse than rotten eggs.

Will turned to run, and Frank started to back away, urging them to follow. "I think we'd best be leaving," insisted Evan.

"I couldn't agree more," stated Eric, who placed his hand on Mike's shoulder.

Mike looked back at them and pulled the orange flare pistol from his jacket, meeting their gaze. "The smell—it's methane!"

Both Eric and Evan quickly nodded, and Mike gripped the gun with both hands, and pointed it towards the hole, now furiously venting gases. He pulled the trigger. Ka-Chunk!

The three saw the glowing projectile fly into the center of the stage, then bounce into the hole as they turned to run. The now thunderous moan stopped instantly, and time appeared to crawl to a standstill.

KRA-KOOM!!

Almost 100 yards away Frank and Will saw the forest turn into day. The sound of the blast hurt their ears, followed by a blast wave visible as it upset leaves around them.

Frank and Will made their way back to the ruined compound, where dozens of small fires burned around the massive wreck of what used to be the circular hall. The ground underneath the structure appeared to have slumped further, forming a larger pit that encapsulated the burning remains.

They located Evan first, then Eric, beaten and bleeding from the ears

74

but alive, and finally Mike as well under a section of broken pew. Dazed and similarly bloody, the three were able to limp back to the car with Frank and Will's help.

"What the hell was that... back there?" yelled Evan. They glanced at each other, attempting to reconcile what they had just encountered.

"...Barbara?" Eric whispered.

DAMN THE CREEK

Gary and Todd made their way past the blackberry bushes, still months away from producing any fruit. This was the first landmark they passed as they entered the scrub, an area that couldn't decide between woods and field. Gary wondered why tall trees hadn't yet taken hold in this area, their scarcity showcasing the clouds overhead.

Todd whacked at the thicket ahead with a makeshift walking stick he had removed from a downed maple branch earlier. Gary felt the first raindrops since they had been walking but wasn't fazed, as it had been sprinkling on and off the last few days. This late in the spring it was warm but not yet muggy, and the ground foliage was almost filled in, the trees occupied once more by countless leaves.

School was almost out for the two, with only a week left of their first year of middle school. Summer was almost within grasp, when getting up early and homework could finally take a hike. The two had been friends since Todd's family moved to town a few years prior, and they hung out often. Weather over the winter and early spring had kept them mostly indoors, but with the recent violent thunderstorms having subsided, they weren't going to let a little rain keep them from going out to explore.

Gary had brought a pullover but removed it to cool down and tied it around his waist. Todd had on his usual jean jacket, and Gary could see raindrops beginning to register on the blue fabric. Gary was no stranger to these woods, and was reminded of this when they passed by a chunk of milky white granite that jutted from the weeds.

He had grown up going on regular walks and hikes with his dad since he was a toddler, and he remembered the first time they had passed the granite, likely at age five. He initially thought it was ice, based on its appearance, "but how could there still be ice so long after winter?" He shook his head at the memory.

The vegetation grew taller as they stepped once more into forest, the canopy providing light protection from the rain. Once inside it was hard to tell if the rain was picking up or just drops of water were passing from leaf to leaf. Either way, the subtle pitter-patter was always a soothing sound. They picked up a game trail, widened by human use but identifiable as animal-made by its meandering direction.

They were spurred on by a desire to see the effect of the recent rains on the creeks and streams within the forest, what areas might have flooded or what banks may have given way. The waterways were always a highlight in any hiking excursion, but usually following a spring deluge, surprises were to be expected.

They soon found their way to a larger trail, and followed it over the undulating forest floor, littered with Mayapple and several types of ferns. The trail was packed enough to not be slippery from waterfall unless you were on an incline or were near the occasional puddle. A variety of mushrooms pushed up from the floor of last year's leaves. Gary knew enough about fungi from his dad—don't handle any of them unless you are an expert. Fortunately Todd hadn't challenged him on the subject.

Up ahead lay the first tributary worth checking. Gary had pulled crayfish from the various pools along it years ago; as a result he informally named it Crayfish Creek. It seemed to begin further up the gentle slopes, where he rarely investigated, as the action began where you could see actual streambed. There appeared to be a reasonable flow of water, at least several inches deeper than normal but nothing impressive yet.

They followed the bank of Crayfish Creek as the contour of the land deepened, and soon they were nestled between two sloping hills covered in ash, hickory and maple trees. Ahead, the valley intersected with a larger creek, though Gary had no name for it.

Higher on the hill that terminated between the convergence of the two creeks sat an old oak tree, one of the thickest trees Gary knew of in the forest, with a diameter of at least six feet at its base. It still had one low hearty branch in such a spot that Gary's dad had once been able to secure a rope over its reach. Dangling over the edge of the hill, Gary and his friends had been able to swing on the rope far out over the gully below, providing for a thrilling ride.

The gully was that of the unnamed stream, which was babbling along with a more impressive volume of water than Crayfish Creek, the water flowing smooth and almost a foot deep in places. The gravel banks revealed debris from heavier flow, when the regular bank couldn't handle the additional runoff. Several small ponds punctuated the flow of the stream, with mini waterfalls scattered throughout.

Muddy banks, left exposed and eroded, revealed countless roots from the forest floor above, its edge overhanging haphazardly. Occasional bands of gray and brown clay could be seen at the deeper levels of exposed bank near the waterline. The sprinkles had turned to a light rain, but depending on where you walked, various treetops provided adequate cover.

Gary began checking the larger pond where the two creeks met. He spied numerous minnows, some slightly larger than the size of a finger, and true to the initial creek's name, several crayfish creeping along the bottom. Todd had stepped over to the other side of the creek and was flipping flat rocks along the edge with his stick.

As the rain picked up, so too did the collective flow within the streams; they could see minor puddles growing and temporary blockages overcome with the increased flow. By now they were mostly soaked, so when they simultaneously arrived at the idea of altering the water flow, they removed their socks and shoes and rolled up their pant legs.

Todd began dragging a downed log south of the convergence, and Gary scooped up a few larger rocks above the waterline. They set up a crude barrier which quickly sprung leaks as water flowed and eroded their initial attempts.

Surveying the gradual slope of terrain and embankments, they began crafting a more substantial wall well above the pool, reinforced with rocks and handfuls of muddy clay. Enough fallen debris lay about that they were able to drag or carry with ease, except for a larger log they both had to coerce into place.

They built up their dam with an opening in the center for water to flow during construction. When they finally plugged this remaining hole, they laughed at the overkill of their endeavor. While only a few feet high in places, the makeshift structure spanned over thirty feet across the valley basin.

"It's too bad we don't have a camera," Todd remarked, and Gary thought about the Instamatic back at his house, wondering if there was any film left over.

"This is the biggest thing I've ever made," Todd added.

"What am I, chopped liver?" Gary complained in a mocking tone.

"You know, we made," Todd corrected.

The muddy pond began to slowly fill as they waded knee-deep in places to shore up sections and plug any leaks. The effort had left them drenched but satisfied, and the rain appeared to finally let up as if to mock their efforts. After admiring their collaborative efforts in creating a pond roughly fifteen feet in diameter, they decided to call it a day.

That night and into the next day the rain returned, heavy at times, and Gary spent the day in school wondering if the dam had held or might need to be repaired. On the bus ride home Todd was curious as well but more motivated to look for a pocketknife that had slipped from his pocket. "My grandpa gave it to me," He explained.

They met up an hour later with rain gear and began the trek to their dam. The rain was heavy at times and the path was riddled with numerous puddles, and instead of the Crayfish Creek approach, they followed the hill to the old oak tree overlooking their dam.

They both gasped in incredulity, as the entire basin had filled in, stretching over sixty feet at its widest. Finally Todd let out a nervous laugh and they heard a loud SPLASH! from the bank below. They exchanged curious glances and attempted to peer over the hill's edge, hanging on to the oak tree's trunk.

"Do you think the bank is giving way?" Todd asked

"If it is, it's probably not a good idea for us to hang around up here," Gary answered, and they crept laterally around the slope further upstream. Eventually they found a place to cross and made way to the opposite side of their pond. "There, look," Gary pointed to a section of bank composed of clay far below the oak that had collapsed, though it was almost completely submerged. The pond was an opaque brown except for near the higher banks, where grayish murk was introduced by the disturbed clay layers.

"Sheesh, we're not going to get in trouble for this, are we?" Todd wondered.

"Of course not, it's just the woods, goofball," Gary reminded with a chuckle.

"Oh yeah, right," Todd acknowledged and began taking off his boots as the rain increased.

"You're still going in?" Gary asked.

"Yeah, not that far, I just have to find my pocketknife. It's probably right where I put my shoes yesterday." Todd pointed at a place roughly a dozen feet from the edge of the shore they stood upon.

"I don't know if that's a good idea. You can't even see the bottom. What are you gonna do, use your feet to find it?" Gary stared down at Todd's bare feet in the mud, and noticed deer tracks nearby filling with water.

Todd was having second thoughts when a nearby FLASH surprised them, followed rapidly by an explosive CRACK of thunder. The two swore as Todd shoved his feet back into his boots, "That was too close!" Todd shouted, and they both knew it was time to go, and scrambled back over the stream and up the hill towards the oak.

"Not too close!" Gary yelled in reference to the massive tree, thinking it might be the lightning storm's next target. They high-tailed it home in the downpour, hurried along by additional flashes and thunder cracks, finally collapsing in Gary's garage in a fit of nervous laughter.

With the final days of school, their attention was diverted for the remainder of the week. It wasn't until the following Sunday that they were able to return to their dam and attempt to locate Todd's pocket knife.

In the near week since their last visit, the forest had pretty much dried out; along the trail they encountered the remnants of only one major puddle. The sunlight that filtered down through the canopy above provided stark contrast from their last visit. The ground cover appeared even more dense and vibrant, and a hint of humidity hung in the air.

Following the Crayfish Creek approach, they were amused to see their dam still intact, even if the water level had dropped significantly. The pond was nearly the size of the first day again, about twenty five feet across. The basin told the history of the backflow however, as all of the plants and ground that were underwater at the peak were tinged with a coating of the brownish silt, the same color as the remaining opaque pond.

Todd circled around and began searching through the bank. "Do you see it yet?" Gary called out from the other side, after briefly checking Crayfish Creek for any of its namesake inhabitants. There were none immediately evident.

"Not yet. I was thinking, maybe we drain it a little," Todd suggested.

"Oh, you mean dismantle the dam?" Gary responded, thought for a few moments, then shrugged in agreement. "Next time we can make it even bigger!" he declared as they stepped past the retaining wall and began pulling out branches and debris from a center section.

After struggling for a few minutes with a stubborn log, a large enough section gave way to produce a steady flow of murky water downstream. Gary and Todd returned to the most likely spot for the pocketknife and waited for the water level to recede.

"What is that, a branch?" Todd asked, pointing to the center of the pond. Gary's attention was elsewhere.

"Todd, look over there." Gary motioned to the bank directly below the oak tree, and they approached for a better look. The drainage had exposed a large under hang, an unnaturally smooth discolored cavity in the gray clay layer large enough for them both.

"Think the tree's going to fall?" Todd asked, referring to the oak further above. Gary looked up the slope at the old tree, thinking of all it had seen in its long life.

With a splash the central wall of the dam collapsed and the drainage accelerated as the creek downstream struggled to contain the surge of murky water. Todd returned his attention to the branch. "That's not a branch," he said, answering his earlier question.

"I think that's… an antler," Gary replied in a puzzled tone. Flecks of sunlight dappled across the muddy prongs of a lone antler poking above the surface, first three tines then four as the water drained.

By the time the deer's skull and rib cage had broken the surface, the skeletal remains of at least a dozen more indeterminate animal carcasses were visible, scattered throughout the muck. All of the bones appeared to have been chewed upon.

Gary thought back to the SPLASH! last week, exactly where the cavity lay beneath the oak tree.

He realized they hadn't been alone at the dam since then.

As the boys ran off, a pair of unblinking eyes watched from the deepest muck. No one saw it crawl out over the remains of the dam and slither downstream… in search of *larger* prey.

THE TALENT SHOW

Heather hated this part of the day. The softball game everyone was required to participate in wouldn't have been so bad if she was better at it. But she wasn't very good at catching or hitting, nor did she find any it interesting. She wasn't too sure she was good at anything yet. But as bad as the current activity was, it was nothing compared to what was yet to occur following supper - the talent show.

It was day two of the camp getaway her entire class was attending, where each sixth grade goes for about a week. Set in an old-growth forest, the two hour bus ride would give them the opportunity to 'get close to nature.'

In order to attend, each student had to peddle six boxes of chocolate bars in order to pay for the cost of the trip. Initially having a difficult time selling beyond her neighbors and family members, Heather had been saved when her father took her to work one day and 'enlisted' the aid of his co-workers.

She stood in the outfield, hoping no one would hit the ball in her direction, while kids yelled back and forth and several counselors tried to keep things civil. If the ball never came, she could get through this, but there would be no dodging the talent show, unless she feigned sickness or hid. As she dreaded the idea of performing in front of her class, Heather began thinking of a good hiding place around the camp, ruling out the cabins, the bathrooms or — WHACK!

A fly ball headed her way, and she suddenly heard a dozen of her classmates yelling her name. She made a valiant effort to predict where the ball might fall, but failed miserably and the ball bounced yards behind her towards the dense treeline.

She ran after the ball as the urging of her classmates changed in tone as she knew she was letting everyone down. The ball landed several feet shy of the trees and as she was about to grab it a loud KRACK! startled her. The distant sound echoed in the hills and forest beyond and Heather's first thought was that of fireworks - she knew some of the boys had brought a batch, having secretly noticed their discrete show and tell on the bus ride out.

Having paused momentarily, she heard her classmates resume calling out her name, and she scooped up the ball from the grass. She turned and threw the ball fast and roughly where it needed to go, surprising herself if only briefly.

KRACK! KRACK! More explosive noises from the forest distracted everyone from Heather's throw, and one of the counselors began blowing a whistle. A half a dozen more KRACKs followed in rapid succession and it became clear to Heather that they weren't firecrackers. The whistling counselor was signaling everyone to come in from the field.

Clusters of her classmates were talking to each other by the backstop, and when Heather passed by two counselors speaking in hushed tones she distinctly overheard the word 'gunshots?'. Several more

KRACKs rang out, echoing from an indeterminate location.

"Everyone—get with your cabin group…" Counselor Duncan called out with her hands in the air, repeating several times to be heard over the chatter. Camp Director Mr. Burton put his whistle to use once more, repeating what Miss Duncan had been saying.

Heather scanned the crowd for her bunk mates and found Jennifer, Madeline and the rest of her group assembling, while overhearing variations on "What was that?", "What are we doing?" amongst her classmates as she made her way to her cabin group.

Mr. Burton nodded in agreement with several of the other counselors and announced to the group, "Let's everyone return to their cabins, and get ready for supper." Individual counselors began shepherding the groups back to their cabins. Heather trailed her group and watched Mr. Burton linger behind and stare back at the baseball field and forest beyond.

Within a minute they filed back into their cabin ushered by their designated Counselor, Miss Price, who managed to distract them with questions about the talent show, though Heather wasn't fooled. She could tell Miss Price was trying to keep them calm and occupied while she made sure they were all present. From Heather's bunk she could see Mr. Burton in front of the administrative cabin with several counselors and other camp staff.

"What are you going to do for the talent show, Heather?" Madeline asked from the next bunk over.

Jennifer walked over and leaned against Heather's bunk. "I'll be singing a song from the play—" KRACK! Another distant shot rang from outside, and Heather saw the staff disperse out the window.

"Miss Price, what's that noise out there?" asked Becky, another of their cabin mates.

"Oh, that's nothing to worry about Becky, just someone playing tricks," Miss Price explained, and was interrupted from further explanation by a knock at the cabin door. She greeted Counselor Duncan, who after exchanging a few words in hushed tones, promptly left. Heather got off her bunk to peer out the other side of the room to see Miss Duncan already arriving at the next cabin.

"Girls—let's get ready for supper," Miss Price clapped her hands and announced to the cabin, while repeatedly checking her watch.

"I guess we'll be eating early tonight," Madeline remarked.

"Can we go wash up?" Jennifer asked Miss Price repeatedly, as Heather pulled on a gray hooded sweatshirt.

"Pretty soon, Jenny, are you dressed for supper?" Miss Price answered curtly.

"It's Jennifer," Jennifer corrected under her breath. Madeline chuckled as she tied her sneakers.

Heather kept an eye out her window as the daylight ebbed, and within a few minutes she saw Miss Duncan return to the administrative cabin.

"Who do you think is going to win the talent show?" Becky asked Madeline.

"Probably Johnny, he's really good with juggling—who do you think is going to win? Madeline replied. Before she could answer Miss Price announced they would be heading over to the dining hall immediately.

As the group was led briskly to the dining hall, they were joined by the other cabin groups and counselors. They passed by the A-frame administrative cabin nestled under white pine and taller sugar maple trees, and inside Heather could see Mr. Burton on the phone.

Within a few minutes they were inside the dining hall, the largest structure on the property. The interior was built of old-fashioned timbers and reminded Heather of a barn with windows. There were about a dozen picnic benches arranged in three rows, a large section devoted to the kitchen, and a stage situated at the far end, framed by storage closets.

The children were encouraged to find their seats as the kitchen staff went to work, initially handing out small snack bags. Counselors were having a conference near the front doors, a small line formed at the only indoor bathroom, while the hall was filled with the noise of several dozen sixth graders.

Heather left her table full of talk of 'who might win the talent contest' as she took a seat nearby the counselors and pretended to eat her pretzels, hoping to overhear anything they weren't telling.

After a few minutes they started serving food as she was losing interest, when she heard the car pull up. Her classmates lined up for hamburgers and fries as several of the counselors went outside. Heather got up for a peek at the nearest window and saw a state police vehicle parked nearby.

Outside she could see the trooper talking with Mr. Burton, illuminated in the dusk by the amber of the camp lights.

"Heather! Go line up and get yourself something to eat," Miss Price insisted. Before Heather left the window she saw the trooper switch on a powerful flashlight and head towards the baseball field.

"Miss Price, is everything ok?" Heather inquired.

"Of course it is, dear, he's just making sure everyone is safe," Miss Price leaned in close. "To be honest, I'd be more worried about the hamburgers. My recommendation is for the fish sandwich, but they run out quick, so you better hurry," She added with a wink.

The remaining Counselors entered the dining hall followed by Mr. Burton, while Heather picked up a tray and got in line. She realized she was a little bit hungry, and decided to go with Miss Price's suggestion about the fish.

The Counselors were joking and approaching Heather to join in line, when the front doors burst open, and a stranger wearing a plaid coat charged in, quickly closing the doors behind him.

"Ha—ha—have to hide!" He mumbled, frantically pulling a nearby cabinet in front of the doors.

The din of the Hall lowered as all eyes were upon the stranger, and Mr. Burton, bolstered by another male counselor, cautiously approached the man. "Excuse me, Sir—Sir—Can I help you?"

The man gazed at Mr. Burton with wild eyes, nearly out of breath and sweating profusely. "Can we talk—outside, for the children's sake?" Mr. Burton offered, his hands outstretched in an attempt to calm the man.

"Outside?!" The man gasped, as several GUNSHOTS rang out from the far side of the camp. The hair stood up on the back of Heather's neck, conversations stopped and several of her classmates recoiled with alarm. "We shot it too…" The stranger whispered.

The room went quiet. Heather slowly set her tray down on a nearby table that was occupied by a few classmates, the nearest a thin boy named Jimmy and tugged on his sleeve as she crept under the table. The boy looked at her oddly for a moment then got the hint, and he too crawled underneath.

The stillness was broken by the sound a final SHOT, a brief YELL, followed by a GUTTURAL HOLLERING MOAN that sent the room into panic.

"What the hell was that?!" counselor Duncan groaned, while other counselors struggled to react. Heather's classmates started shouting, some scrambling to the back closets, while a few followed Heather's example and crawled under tables. "Is it a bear?" She heard someone yell from under the next table.

"We... TRIED to shoot it too," trembled the Stranger.

"Everyone calm down! Don't Panic!" Shouted Mr. Burton at the room, as the stranger ran towards the center of the hall and huddled between tables. Outside came the sound of wood splintering, sparks flew past one of the windows, and the lights flashed once...

...before going OUT.

In the darkness Heather heard several screams, sobbing from frightened classmates, others in hysterics. "Everyone get down!" Heather heard a nearby counselor call out.

"Hush! Everyone, stay where you are and be quiet!" called out Mr. Burton, who she heard crouching nearby.

Heather's eyes adjusted to the darkness, aided by the red glow of an exit sign. She started to pick out classmates within the room, hearing a familiar voice sobbing nearby. She crawled out from under her table as Jimmy whispered "Don't go!" and crept over to a crying girl.

"Becky—you'll be safer under here," Heather coaxed the girl to crawl beneath her table, lessening her audible sobs.

"What do we do?" Counselor Duncan begged nearby.

"A call—we need to call for—" Mr. Burton stammered anxiously, interrupted by Miss Price from across the room. "The pay phone here is out—maybe the phone in admin!?"

"Uh, yeah—or the police car, the radio...!" Mr. Burton asserted, as a LOUD CRASH of metal twisting issued from outside. Mr. Burton crept over to the nearest window. "The car is... it's..."

Mr. Burton slumped beneath the window. Counselor Duncan maneuvered closer and peeked over the sill. "It's gone!" She gasped, then recoiled and ducked. "There's... something...out there" She whispered, as Heather pulled her hood over her head.

"What is it?" Mr. Burton mumbled as the cries subsided within the room.

"We saw it," the Stranger spoke blankly. "In the sandpit. We didn't think it was... *real.*"

A shadow passed by one of the windows. "It can't be real. We shouldn't... have shot it."

Screams issued from the room near another window. "There!" A boy cried out, as a shape briefly filled the next window. The room fell silent, and Heather realized she was holding her breath. She didn't want to look at the windows. "Make it go away," came a whimper from elsewhere in the room.

From the rafters above there was a knock followed by a few thumps. A thunk near the window sounded closest to Heather. She didn't want to look. She took shallow breaths, realized her knees were shaking. Becky screamed, and Heather accidentally glanced towards the window.

A SINGLE GIANT EYE STARED BACK, the remainder of its face obscured by the window frame.

Heather clenched her eyes shut and immediately put her head down. More brief cries indicated the window had cleared, as Heather found herself thinking of being anywhere but here. "Did you see it?" A boy two tables down called out. Moments passed, and Heather heard vague whispers around her.

Moments turned to minutes. "Is it gone?" A voice broke the silence. Counselor Duncan peeked over a windowsill. Mr. Burton did the same at another.

"I don't hear anything," Miss Price called out in hushed tones.

Whispered conversations slowly filled the room as panic began to subside. Heather opened her eyes but avoided the window. Accustomed to the dim light, she could see most of her classmates huddled under tables, with the Counselors near the windows and the Stranger crouched between tables in the middle of the room, his eyes glued to the windows.

"We have to get to the phone," Counselor Duncan whispered.

"Yeah," Mr. Burton nodded and crept over to the front door. "Help me move this cabinet—quietly," He beckoned to Counselor Duncan.

Heather saw the Stranger notice and recoil. "What?!" He rose to his feet. "Don't open that door!" He charged the front—SMASH! Glass shards exploded into the room, as something erupted through a window—

AN IMPOSSIBLY LONG ARM,

with spindly fingers that grabbed the Stranger mid-stride, CLUTCHING as he began to scream, that then VIOLENTLY pulled him from their midst.

Hysterical SCREAMS filled the dining hall.

Struggling to breathe, Heather tried to scream. She was one of the few who heard the stranger screaming up on the roof over the panic inside. Even after she pressed her palms over her ears, his shrieks continued far too long.

Emergency crews had arrived by dawn, with ambulances and a state trooper presence that would make anyone feel secure.

There was some initial delay when escorting Heather's class from the dining hall, as each were covered with blankets and given strict instructions:

"DO NOT LOOK BACK AT THE ROOF."

THE VALLEY

Kyle switched off the engine. He'd pulled onto a service road and driven for about half a mile until he reached the treeline ahead. He stepped out of the green Blazer and pulled on his gloves, his breath visible in the crisp air.

The sun had set a few hours prior, and though the moon wasn't visible through the clouds, the thin crust of snow provided enough bounce illumination to see. Up ahead was the reason for his visit, a metal gate he'd regularly check after sundown to check for any late hunters, as hunting ended just after sunset.

As a game warden of only six months for Medina County, he'd drawn the short straw when it came to working holidays, as would be the case until someone else was hired. Until then he didn't mind, with the exception of this evening, tonight being Christmas Eve.

His knew his wife would be waiting with their infant daughter, hopefully with her ham and cabbage dish, and he looked forward to spending the night and following day with them.

Approaching the metal gate, he checked the latch and removed his glove to retrieve a key from his pants pocket. He opened the large padlock, and then closed the lock securing the latch. There were no tire tracks on the snow but a pair of footprints on the road caught Kyle's eye. The tracks only entered the woods and he judged them to be recent based on their crispness in the snow.

Either hunters or hikers, must've exited another route… Kyle thought to himself, and paused briefly to put his glove back on. Still, though he had been the subject of tests and pranks as the new guy, this wasn't enough to arouse his suspicion, until he heard the report of gunfire, a single distant shot. It was unlikely anyone was target practicing this evening, and deer hunting was over several hours ago.

He retrieved a flashlight from the blazer and stepped around the gate, following the footsteps into the forest. Though a native of Ohio, he had grown up in the southern portion of the state and received his degree from Hocking College with the loose intent of becoming a Park Ranger.

Soon after graduating he'd completed a job application with the Ohio Department of Natural Resources, who contacted him about an opening for a Game Warden. The position up north offered more money, and with a new family he gladly accepted the offer.

Fortunately he'd completed enough requirements to qualify, and didn't mind the mild career deviation, or possible course correction, as he thought back to hiking through the woods with his father some fifteen years ago.

It was a winter day when they'd hiked several miles back to a frozen lake, testing the ice with their hiking sticks before venturing onto the surface. They slid around for a short while until a muffled crack had them departing. As they were headed back and laughing at their 'near death experience', they came across a deer.

In a clearing between three large trees lay the animal, dead as anything Kyle had ever seen. From the blood on the snow's surface, it had been killed either that day or the previous. The part that didn't make sense to his young mind was the absence of the deer's head.

Later his Father explained that there were hunters, poachers, and then another sort—those responsible for what they had found. It was a seminal moment for Kyle, the idea that the environment, and by default the wildlife within, were worth protecting.

His attention snapped back to the footsteps as he followed them over a crest and into the forest, his eyes scanning through the vertical lines of countless tree trunks. A snowflake dropped into view, followed by countless more.

Barely a flurry, he thought to himself, and continued over the undulating terrain to the edge of a large valley, its slope dropping in elevation a few hundred feet to a creek bed below.

He switched off his flashlight and surveyed the terrain below, hampered slightly by the light snowfall. He heard them before he saw them, two voices from the distant end of the valley. He traversed the ridge until he was within sight of the two individuals. As it was never a good idea to surprise anyone with a gun, let alone a possible poacher, he stood behind a tree, switched on his flashlight, and announced his presence.

"Game Warden! I need to check your licenses!" He rested his other hand on the revolver at his hip hoping this wouldn't be the first time he'd need it. "Game Warden!" He repeated, and heard the faint echo of his shout return.

"Yeah! Don't shoot Warden!" came a voice from the valley below, followed by a cough and another voice he couldn't make out.

"I have to check your licenses," He shouted, and observed them for a few moments to check for any suspicious movement. Satisfied, he made his way down the hillside, using available trees both for slope assistance and potential cover.

He reached the bottom of the slope without incident and shined his flashlight ahead at the two men, each with rifles slung over their backs. They walked slowly towards him and he got a good look at the two. Though shorter than Kyle, the taller of the duo wore a patterned flannel coat, and appeared to be in his fifties. The other wore a muffler style cap and a tan corduroy jacket and was the source of the coughing.

"Evening gentlemen," Kyle greeted as the light flurry developed into a regular snowfall. Had the snow arrived any sooner their tracks would have been obscured, he thought to himself.

"Howdy Warden, how can we help ya," Flannel acknowledged with a gravelly voice.

"I need to check your hunting licenses, also remind that hunting is legal until one half hour after dark," Kyle asserted, as a breeze began pushing the falling snow diagonally.

"Oh, we're not hunting, just doing some target shooting, er… Warden," Flannel assured and his partner nodded. Without evidence of a kill, Kyle knew challenging the men at their word was not necessary, whether he believed them or not.

"Alright well, even though it is after hours I highly recommend you consider wearing some hunter orange for safety's sake, which I won't write you a ticket for, but I will need to see some ID," Kyle requested with a friendly but guarded tone.

Flannel squinted and cracked a grin, then patted his pockets. "ID? I'm afraid I must've left my wallet in my other pants; otherwise I'd be happy to oblige. Name's Earl Pike and that there is Teddy," he motioned to his friend, who nodded and coughed. "Theodore Hutchins. But everybody calls me Teddy," He clarified with a clearing of his throat.

The falling snow was growing heavy, and the wind started to pick up, stinging Kyle's face with each gust.

"Other than Warden, is there another name we can call you by?" Earl cupped his gloveless hands over his mouth, exhaled and rubbed them together. "Kinda feel like I'm in prison," He added with a chuckle.

"Officer Porter is fine. Pike and Hutchins, that's good enough for paperwork," Kyle jotted down their names on a notepad, swiping away flakes of snow from the surface with his gloved hand.

"I'll let you get going before we lose visibility, so I'll bid you two a good evening," Kyle stuffed the notepad and pencil into his jacket pocket, and gave a parting nod.

"Obliged Mr. Porter, God be with you," Pike raised his hand and Hutchins gave a small wave as Kyle decided to walk further back up the bed of the valley before climbing the slope up and out. Glancing occasionally back he saw them once before the snowfall completely obscured them.

The wind became more persistent, and he could swear he felt the sting of individual snowflakes on his face as he trudged through a layer of accumulating snow. In spite of keeping his head tucked down against the wind, he spotted an agreeable incline and pathway up ahead.

The density of snow falling eased though the wind showed no sign of lessening. In the brief lull Kyle could see barren treetops high above swaying violently.

A few steps up the slope his feet slipped out from under him and he fell forward, a layer of snow breaking his fall. Using the trunk of a nearby sapling for support he pulled himself to his feet when a dark shape caught his eye a few yards away on the valley bed.

Obscured from his approach view earlier lay the carcass of a doe surrounded by mini snow drifts, the stain of crimson still evident on and under the fresh powder. Adrenaline immediately surged through Kyle's veins, and he crouched and drew his pistol, certain they had known he would locate their quarry.

A heavy gust of wind hit Kyle from behind and he struggled to remain standing, as the flurries returned en masse. He rose to his feet and began doubling back to where he had last seen Earl and Ted, and found himself surrounded in thick blizzard conditions, the wind furiously howling around him.

Kyle struggled to navigate in the near whiteout, attempting to discern vertical shapes from the pale ambiguity all around, at last spotting two shadowy shapes fleeing in the distance. He crouched behind a tree and shouted, but could barely hear himself over the wind blasting through the valley.

Rising in intensity to a thunderous roar and certain a tornado was on his heels, Kyle glanced behind momentarily at the furious howling and roaring -

The blizzard was alive and moving in ways impossible, clustering and forming shapes. Pouring down from the sky and charging into the basin of the valley, the furiously churning mass buffeted Kyle as he huddled tight against his tree.

Holding a hand to cover his face, through his fingers he saw outlines of... animals? Improbable as it was, he first saw the paws and shape of a wolf running, a massive stag or elk bounding, a bear charging and countless other similar amorphous shapes above the ground, all formed from snow and wind.

The mass surged past him and soon engulfed the shadowy figures ahead, and against his better judgment Kyle ran forward to another tree trunk to hear the shrieks of the two poachers joining the roaring and howling, obscured in a swirling stampede of solid white, coalescing around them.

Gradually the winds subsided, and soon only mild gusts remained to distribute the falling snow. Kyle cautiously approached where the men had been, and searched thoroughly until his extremities were numb, but could find no sign of the two, the wind and snow scouring and obscuring any remaining trace.

At last returning to the truck he ran the heater for almost half an hour while he tried to make sense of what he had just witnessed, let alone dare report. Unsure if contacting law enforcement was the next step, he drove home and instead decided to call his supervising officer once he'd parked in his driveway.

Gathering his thoughts, he radioed the individual who had trained him through his probationary period, an aged salt-of-the-earth man named Abner who had subsequently retired. After apologizing for contacting late on this holiday evening, he related an abridged version of the story, omitting mention of the spectral wildlife.

There was a long pause after Kyle finished. "Earl Pike and Ted Hutchins, near the East Branch you say?" crackled the radio at last. Kyle acknowledged, unsure of the tone in Abner's voice. He was certain of what he had witnessed, at least until the… stampede? Kyle shook his head, he was pretty sure he didn't believe in -

"Did you see... animals?" His former supervisor inquired. Kyle held his breath as he saw his wife peer through the curtain in front of his house, Christmas lights blinking around the window's perimeter.

"Yeah," He eventually answered.

"Earl Pike and Ted Hutchins went missing over thirty, almost forty years ago, also on a Christmas Eve if I remember. We found 'em in the spring thaw, but by then there wasn't much left to find," Abner explained, his voice switching to a whisper over the radio:

"You've probably heard of the 'Great Hunt of 1818', where the locals exterminated all wildlife in the area? That was also on Christmas Eve. You didn't hear it from me, but that valley... it doesn't forget."

SEVENTEEN

Still only fifteen years old, there weren't a lot of employment options available to Stephanie. There was the occasional babysitting for the Myford's down the street, but that was too sporadic, and as their son got older, the less they needed a sitter.

She couldn't wait to turn sixteen and get an actual job like her friend Krystal. Krystal had picked up a crappy job that summer working at one of the burger joints in town, but at least it was a job. Stephanie was eager to continue saving for Art College—still a few years away—a custom her parents had instilled in her early.

When her father lost his job at the steel factory last year, Stephanie was determined not to add to their financial troubles, as she was aware they were still trying to catch up with less income.

It was Krystal, who on her day off, already tired of her job and perusing the want ads in the local newspaper, had came across an ad for an 'ARTIST WANTED. P/T $20 per drawing.' Also listed was a phone number. She immediately shared it with Stephanie.

"What does PT mean?" She asked Krystal.

"Oh, that's part time," she replied while fussing with her curly blonde hair in Stephanie's vanity mirror.

"Drawings of what?" Stephanie wondered aloud as she scrutinized the tiny ad.

"Who cares? Twenty bucks is twenty bucks. Right now it takes me six, seven hours to make that, and I know how fast you are with your sketches. Those were the only thing that got me through seventh period study hall. Besides, you want to be an artist, right? Just remember me when you're big and famous," she kidded, and spritzed hairspray into her curls.

Before Krystal left to meet her boyfriend, Stephanie assured her she would call the number before her parents got home. She'd put off the call until Krystal left so she could attempt a 'professional' voice, and knew the presence of her friend might make that a challenge, given Krystal's penchant for practical jokes.

As she dialed the number and sat down at the kitchen table with a pen and tablet, she heard her parent's car in the driveway. "Hello?" an elderly male voice answered the phone.

Stephanie cleared her throat. "Um, Hi yes, I'm calling about the artist wanted ad?" Her parents walked into the kitchen, immediately saw that she was on the phone, and silently mouthed greetings to her. Stephanie pointed out the ad to her mother as her father went to the garage.

"Artist wanted? Ah yes, I do want an artist. I'd like someone to produce some drawings for a book I'm working on. They'll need to be detailed, and suitable for print. Is that something you're interested in?" the elderly man asked.

"Detailed drawings for a book? Um yes. I'm very interested,"

Stephanie responded.

"Ok, well I'll need to see some samples. Can you send a photocopy of some of your artwork?" Also, I should point out one thing first —the drawings are of... insects. Will that be an issue, young lady?"

Stephanie inhaled audibly. She was none too fond of creepy-crawlies, and against her first instinct she replied, "No... not a problem." She held her breath.

"Ah good. My name is Charles Burchill..." He spelled out his last name, and Stephanie repeated his name aloud, drawing her mother's attention.

"Mr. Burchill? Stephanie, let me interrupt you," her mother held her hand out for the phone.

Stephanie managed a, "Hold on." before handing the phone over. Clearly her mother knew him.

"Mr. Burchill, this is Stephanie's mom, Joan, Joan Tipton. How are you doing?" Stephanie's thoughts turned to drawing bugs, wondering what Krystal had gotten her into this time, and overheard something about retirement from her mother's conversation with Mr. Burchill.

Within a few minutes her mother hung up the phone, after having boasted of her daughter's skill and having arranged for an after dinner portfolio visit the next town over with Mr. Charles Burchill. "Oh—Uh, I don't know what to bring," Stephanie said aloud.

"Well, just bring one of your sketchbooks. I'm sure that'll be fine," her mom suggested.

After a rigatoni dinner and hasty artwork selection, Stephanie and her mom drove the winding roads to the Burchill residence. After passing through town, the view alternated between fields, forests and isolated industrial buildings. As they passed a quarry, Stephanie asked how her mother knew Mr. Burchill.

"He was the science teacher when I went to your school. He'd been there for years and retired shortly after I graduated. He was a little bookish, not much of a sense of humor, but otherwise a nice teacher to have. Then again, he did have to put up with my class," her mother mused.

They soon arrived at the residence and were greeted by Mrs. Burchill, a silver-haired elderly woman. "Oh, you must be the artist helping my husband," she greeted Stephanie's mother.

"Actually, my daughter's the artist," her mother clarified.

"Well that's marvelous—won't you both come inside?" She invited them to the living room and went to fetch her husband.

Stephanie sat on the couch next to her mom and looked around. She was reminded of her grandparents house, with pictures covering every wall and with knick-knacks everywhere, all displayed on dark wooden furniture. Many of the mementos appeared to be exotic carved sculptures; she imagined the Burchill's must have traveled the world extensively.

"Hello, Joan! And you must be Stephanie!" Mr. Burchill greeted the two with handshakes, and took a step back to size up Joan with his glasses. "Now I remember you—where has the time gone?" Mr. Burchill took a seat in a recliner opposite the two as they briefly reminisced. Mrs. Burchill interrupted them with a tray of shortbread cookies and offered them glasses of iced tea.

"I understand you've brought along some samples for me to look at?" Mr. Burchill inquired. Stephanie handed over a few pieces of her work, and finally a sketchbook, bookmarked to drawings of elephants she had reproduced from an animal encyclopedia. A mixture of variable width ink lines mixed with pointillist shading, Mr. Burchill stared at the elephants through his bifocals, and then looked up at Stephanie over his lenses. "I think this will do," he said with a smile.

"Now I could go with photos but I think hand-drawn illustrations lend an air of class, to what might otherwise be another stodgy book." Mr. Burchill handed the sketchbook back to Stephanie, and then rose to his feet. "Follow me please. The basement is where the collection is kept. Gertrude's insistence, of course… She refers to it as the 'La-bor-atory'." He drew out the word, in a Karloff-ian voice, as they followed him to the kitchen and cellar door.

Stephanie followed Mr. Burchill down the cellar stairs, while her mom stayed above to chat with Mrs. Burchill. The stairwell was lit with a single incandescent, and Mr. Burchill switched on additional lights once below. A row of fluorescents flashed and hummed as they came to life.

Mounted on the walls above several workbenches were numerous framed glass cases filled with a rainbow display of insects of all sort. Her eyes went first to the butterfly cases, easily the most varied, to the striking array of beetles, the vibrant display of dragonflies, bees, grasshoppers… She had never seen so many specimens in one place and found her feelings of revulsion mixed with curiosity.

"This place is like a museum! How—how long did this take to put together?" She marveled at the countless varieties, all safely deceased and behind glass.

"I suppose I started when I was around your age, and collected from then on. I had always wanted to become an entomologist, but there weren't all that many jobs available as a 'professional bug collector'. So it's been a hobby ever since. A hobby made easier when it comes to collecting specimens; I don't have to travel far. There's an old orchard beyond the backyard. The blossoms there attract all manner of specimens," he explained.

"Now, do you think you can draw these from memory, or would it help to have the subject at hand?" Mr. Burchill asked.

"Uh, not from memory, maybe a picture…" Stephanie muttered.

"Then let's start small, with this wasp and hornet." He handed her a small box with glass lid that contained the two subjects pinned to a dark felt backing.

She took it in hand, stifled a gulp, and stared at the contents of the box. She had been stung in the hand by a wasp when she was six years old, in a toy store reaching for a boxed toy from a shelf. The wasp happened to be on the backside of the product box, and her grasp no doubt angered it as much as it upset her. She'd given a wide berth to anything that buzzed, bit, or had a stinger since then.

"Here—you might need this." She snapped from her memory as he handed her a magnifying glass. "It will help with the details," he added.

Within minutes they had parted ways, and Stephanie sat in the passenger seat as her mom drove home, specimen box in her lap. "Wasps, huh?" her mother commented, cocking an eyebrow.

"Yeah… Wasps," Stephanie sighed.

Within a few days her drawings were complete, and Mr. Burchill was delighted. He gave her two crisp twenty dollar bills in an envelope and her next assignments. This cycle continued for several weeks as she illustrated numerous segmented limbs, thoraxes and antennae.

When delivering her illustrations, Mr. Burchill would point out various bits of trivia concerning each of the subjects of her drawings. "Did you know, the praying mantis is the only insect that can look over its shoulder at you?" he mused, and handed her an open envelope containing several twenty dollar bills for the previous week's dragonfly and cricket drawings.

The more insects she studied and drew, the more she recognized similarities in body structure, and slowly, she came to have an appreciation for the simplicity and commonality of the varying exoskeletons.

Taking the trash to the curb one evening she spotted an odd looking beetle on the ground, and briefly brought it inside for a closer look, an act that she could have scarcely tolerated prior to helping Mr. Burchill with his book. The June bugs common for this time of year were present, but this was something different.

After being dropped off by Krystal on her next visit, she mentioned this to Mr. Burchill, bringing along the specimen she had placed in a small cardboard jewelry box.

"It's curious what you find yourself open to when distracted by other information. I'm going to let you in on a little secret, Stephanie. I'm writing this book as a distraction, a bit of a Trojan horse into academia if you will. And what you brought today, well, that's no beetle, but actually relates directly to my book," he said.

Stephanie's eyes focused on the open jewelry box in Mr. Burchill's hands. "Well, don't keep me in suspense, what do you think it is?" She asked.

"That is the nymph of a cicada, specifically the Magicicada, of the seventeen year variety."

"Like the seventeen year locust?" Stephanie had heard mention of the term years ago, but had paid no attention. Now that she had found one, she was all ears.

"Technically they aren't locusts, but one and the same as you are referring to. You've found an early bird, but soon there will be more, plenty more. This emergence will be the fourth time for me, but this being your first; it's something you'll always remember. That is... assuming they haven't been affected by chemical runoff." His voice trailed off.

"Chemicals—how do you mean affected them?" Stephanie asked.

"Well, they reside underground, living off root fluids most of their life, but in their larval stage they're susceptible to absorbing chemicals present in soil that might interfere with their development. More fertilizers and weed killers have found their way into the ground in the last decade than all previous combined," Mr. Burchill explained.

He motioned with his hand, "Just up the hill, a marvelous lawn, not a weed in sight. Fertilizer company headquarters. Their runoff flows into the old orchard out back, makes the biggest apples you've ever seen, but I might think twice before eating them. So I wonder about the effect on the cicadas," he continued.

"OK, I get it, that's bad. So what's the deal with seventeen years? Why do they wait so long, what's the point —it seems like a waste of time," Stephanie remarked.

"The popular theory was of persistence through climate variations, surviving through poor weather cycles. But I have my own theory… a rather radical one at that—hence the Trojan horse." He said.

"Charles, Stephanie's ride is here!" Gertrude called out from upstairs.

Mr. Burchill quickly collected his thoughts. "Let's discuss cicadas next week, when I imagine we'll be able to locate a mature specimen. I believe my backyard alone will have thousands, not to mention the old orchard. In the meantime, I have two stealthy selections for you: a katydid, and an owl butterfly, two masters of deception," he said, handing her their respective boxes.

During the ride home, Stephanie studied the new subjects, one appearing at first glance to be a green leaf, and the other with bold circular markings on its wings resembling eyes. The camouflage was flawless. "The moth I couldn't miss… but the katydid, there is no way you'd ever see it." she thought to herself.

Within a few days, Stephanie had finished her drawings and began to notice an odd noise outside. As the temperatures increased, so too did the humidity, which served to dampen out anything except for the growing drone, a peculiar sound that reminded her of thousands of tiny washboards being played.

Her parents confirmed the source of the sound as the cicadas, which she soon observed emerging en masse, first in the treeline at the end of their backyard and soon in and around the neighborhood trees.

While getting the mail that week, Stephanie observed the boy she used to babysit out riding his bike. He spotted her and throwing his bike down in her yard, rushed over to greet her, pleading with her to follow him to the base of the small aspen in her front yard. "C'mere! It's a secret!"

She played along, knowing what he'd intended—to shake the tree and freak her out with a shower of loosened cicadas falling from above, which he did. She countered by picking up a pair and telling him they "wanted a kiss" and chasing him back onto his bike and up the street.

She brought one of the cicadas inside, and though Mr. Burchill's official request was still forthcoming, began an illustration of the insect. Finally able to observe their adult form, she was both fascinated yet mildly repulsed. At over two inches long—with transparent yet veined wings, a shiny black carapace, and prominent red eyes—she found them almost sinister in appearance.

Completing the cicada illustration while her mother was still preparing dinner, she joined her father in the living room as he read the paper, while simultaneously listening to the television news. A weatherman teased the possibility of rain for tomorrow, catching her father's attention. "They've been promising rain for the last few weeks… I'll believe it when I see it," he sighed.

Following dinner, Stephanie was inspired to do a second rendition in color of the cicada, this time using markers and colored pencils. As she sat at her drawing table working, her cat kept her company, lounging briefly on the far side of the table before dozing off. Within a few hours she had finished, and she looked forward to showing Mr. Burchill the next day.

Later that night, Stephanie lay in bed, her covers off. The ceiling fan providing little relief from the heat, and she lay in bed that night wishing for a breeze or rainstorm to lower the temperature. Watching distant flashes out her window of an electrical storm illuminating the far off sky, she soon fell asleep, listening to the weird drone of countless 'sinister' bugs outside.

The next day offered no break from the humidity, and after her second shower that day, Stephanie removed the towel from her hair. Finding her curly hair stuck to the back of her neck, she searched her room for an elastic band, ultimately settling on a hair clip. She made a mental note to borrow a scrunchie from Krystal, who always seemed to travel with a mini-salon.

Her day off, Krystal picked Stephanie up on the condition they head to the mall after dropping off her drawings, which she showed her friend in a makeshift portfolio. "Gross—but neat! Now let's get going before I melt! I need a new swimsuit, and you need a break from the bugs... and just maybe we can find you a boyfriend instead!." Krystal teased.

Along the way they drove with the windows down, Stephanie's unclipped hair fluttering in the wind, and they soon arrived at the Burchill residence. As she secured her hair with a borrowed scrunchie, Mrs. Burchill emerged from the front door with a covered dish and shopping bag in hand. "Oh, hello girls, I was just leaving. Canasta night beckons. Charles is out back on another of his safaris." She motioned between the house and garage where a tiled stone path led towards the backyard.

"Ok, thanks. Have a good time!" Stephanie replied, and she and Krystal proceeded. They followed the curving rock-path down the gradual slope of the yard, past mulch lined flower beds, a variety of bushes, and several garden plots. At the bottom of the yard, they passed into what appeared to be a sparse forest, before Stephanie recognized the orderly pattern of the tree placement and remembered the orchard Mr. Burchill had spoken of.

The ground cover was unkempt but not dense, though plenty of saplings and weeds struggled for light from the canopy overhead. A few rotten and fresh apples dotted the ground here and there, and Stephanie spotted a few larger ones hanging low from their branches. The smell reminded her of cider. "What a cool place," Krystal remarked, and Stephanie proceeded to locate her employer.

"Hello, Mr. Burchill. I have some new drawings!" She shouted, pausing to listen for a reply.

She listened briefly, but heard nothing. "Maybe he went back to the house," Krystal offered.

"Yeah, maybe," Stephanie muttered, pausing to listen again, but heard nothing.

'Nothing', she thought. No Mr. Burchill. No birds, no wind, and no… cicadas. Didn't Mr. Burchill expect thousands, and more in the Orchard?

"Hey Steph!" Krystal called out from the next row of trees. She kneeled to pick up a straw hat, and underneath it a journal as Stephanie approached. "Check this out." She handed the book to Stephanie, who juggling with her portfolio, flipped open the book to a natural crease, and silently read:

"It seems my initial assumption about cicadas being able to concentrate toxins is not incorrect. Unfortunately their numbers this cycle have been surprisingly scarce. Of the few I've collected, chemicals found in fertilizer runoff seem to have accumulated in their systems in massive amounts. It doesn't appear to have affected their development other than an average growth of maybe 3 - 5% overall.

"My theory—that they've developed their periodic nature in an evasive response to a specific predator that might also hibernate, sort of a long term hide and seek—may prove to be utter nonsense. Which is just as well, for if there was an organism subsisting entirely on cicadas—specifically this cycles toxic batch—there's no telling if the fertilizer could possibly have a secondary magnifying effect on such a predator."

Stephanie turned the page, continuing to read a more recent entry: "The scarcity isn't due to the chemicals. They've been hunted. I may have made a very serious error. They're mimics—They must have exhausted their preferred prey: the cicada... They're all around me. If I stay very still, I should be able to—"

"Hey Steph, I don't feel a breeze, so why are all the branches moving?" Krystal remarked.

A chill ran up Stephanie's spine.

She raised her head and glanced around, finally squinting to notice among the multitude of oddly swaying branches above, the distinctive segmentation of insect limbs, so common among the subjects of her illustrations.

"Krystal, DO. NOT. MOVE," she hissed to her friend, who immediately caught on that something was... wrong.

Despite the subtle swaying motion, she could see the stick-like limbs slowly clasping further down the tree towards them, almost hypnotic in their subdued approach. As her mind raced she struggled to stay still, then felt the portfolio slowly rotating away, slipping from her grasp. She gripped tighter, but her hold on the journal interfered, and the first of the drawings sailed away.

She held her breath.

The black and white drawing of the cicada landed face up several feet away.

Shrill noises erupted from above, and multiple bundles of 'twigs' fell from the branches. The bundles unfurled and skittered towards the drawing.

They were cut off by the three larger ones that dropped, THumP THunK THUMP, each a yard's worth of branch-like connected limbs.

Chasing off the smaller multiples, mandibles from the three immediately chomped and bit at the cicada image, each competing for the largest piece, soon shredding the drawing.

Their frenzy subsiding, Krystal covered her mouth with both hands, stifling a scream. Stephanie nudged her friend and discreetly showed her the remaining color Cicada illustration still in hand.

Stephanie nodded and silently mouthed, "Get ready to run."

The three soon turned their focus back to the girls, and without a moment to spare she dropped the final color illustration, the last available 'cicada' in the orchard, and with a chorus of shrieks, the trio of branch-mimics LURCHED forward to intercept.

Stephanie and Krystal spun, dropping everything and ran like never before, certain the creatures were right behind them the whole way back to the house, where they scrambled into Krystal's unlocked car and hurriedly rolled up the windows, starting the vehicle and peeling out of the driveway.

Many curse words later, the two drenched with sweat, Stephanie realized the windows were still up and the temperature inside was absolutely sweltering.

They were many miles away before they cracked opened the windows, when the first of the fat raindrops began hitting the windshield.

The low pressure system that rolled in that afternoon failed to yield any verifiable tornadoes, but did produce enough severe winds to knock out power, bring down telephone lines and uproot trees across the county.

It was Krystal who first called the police, but describing 'giant bugs' ended the calls pretty quick.

In the storm's aftermath, Stephanie's parents didn't know what to make of her story, and it was days before they found out indirectly that the Burchill house was severely damaged, the orchard a tangle of broken trees, and Mr. Burchill unaccounted for.

Her parents decided not to pass along Stephanie's story to the authorities.

That autumn, volunteers found Mr. Burchill's remains amidst the tangle of orchard tree debris, and having since moved away, Mrs. Burchill gave Stephanie first dibs on her late husband's insect collection, before donating the rest to a nearby college.

Attending with the help of an art scholarship at the same college, Stephanie later earned dual degrees in art and entomology.

Years subsequent, she published Mr. Burchill's book, giving him full credit, though his theory was derided without evidence.

Stephanie regularly checked a future date in her calendar, crossing off month after month, preparing for a second edition of the book. Counting down from the day in the orchard, she waited.

Seventeen years.

TINKERS

Bill had a song stuck in his head. He'd heard it on the radio earlier that day, and couldn't get rid of it. The worst part was that he didn't know any of the words except for the chorus. He pushed a lawn mower to the song's tempo, and when he reached the property limit, pivoted the mower around for another swath. "Time to turn around, uh-oh," he sung to himself as he pushed the lawn mower through some shade, modifying the chorus to fit his current activity.

He hurried to finish, finally pushing the mower to the edge of the yard where he turned it off and began scraping wet clippings from beneath. Beyond lay the woods, and bright sunlight penetrated the canopy, keeping the mosquitoes at bay. Bill thought it looked like jungle, and at this time of year, he wasn't too far off in his estimation.

The mower scraped clean, he glanced once more at the woods, catching sight of some distant movement. He paused and scanned, finally squinting to spot the source: A single gray squirrel paused on the side of a large sycamore, flitting its tail briefly before scampering to the far side of the trunk. Bill had a bit of a knack for spotting

119

hidden things, whether small animals like squirrels and newts, or limestone fossils from a gravel driveway.

Having finished seventh grade a few weeks prior, his ability to spot the hidden had earned him a few friends that year at his new school. He was in English class one afternoon and spotted a cheat sheet being stealthily circulated around during a test, discovering nearly half the class was in on it.

The cheat sheet was being passed when the fire alarm sounded, and all of the students were quickly being ushered from the room. Bill spotted the sheet fall from the pocket of a red-haired girl. Moments before the teacher spotted the sheet, Bill feigned tying his shoe to pocket it.

After a quick evacuation onto the school grounds, he congregated with his classmates while the rest of the school emptied. He spotted the red-haired girl talking excitedly with a curly blonde girl, and approached them. He stood in front of them and pulled the folded paper from his pocket, quickly unfolded it and handed it to the redhead. "I think you dropped this," he smirked, catching the two by surprise, before the teacher called them to line up for an attendance.

That 'save' earned him their trust, and word soon spread that the new kid was all right. Later that year the red-haired girl saved him from a detention in math class he didn't deserve, and the blonde girl, Chelle, passed word to Bill that a friend was interested in him.

Chelle's friend Gloria was on the quiet side and Bill wasn't exactly a social butterfly himself, but via note passing, Chelle enthusiastically coordinated their interactions. A few weeks and a school dance later their 'going out' had fizzled before going anywhere of significance.

Subsequently Bill and Gloria remained cordial even as they rarely spoke, but Bill had gained a friend in Chelle, who he had no difficulty communicating with.

Chelle had called earlier in the day, with an invite. She, Gloria and a few friends were headed to a local state park later, primarily for swimming in the small lake there.

Acquainted with a few neighborhood boys, he had visited the park a few weeks prior, after their first swimming destination had been dismissed. The first was a small above-ground pool in one of their backyards', but maintenance had been neglected and they found it thick with green algae.

Plans were quickly made to travel to the lake at Tinker's Creek State Park, and Bill found an opportunity to break out his new twelve speed. What was described to him as 'close by' ended up being a several mile trek along rural streets, his longest ride yet. The boy whose family owned the pool complained they should have taken a more direct path through the woods, but was overruled as the rest of the group had street bicycles unsuitable for trails.

While at the park Bill had recognized a few classmates including the red-haired girl, who had relayed to Chelle his presence, leading to today's invite. Bill and Chelle had talked only a few times during the summer break, but this would be their first visit in several months.

Bill's mind snapped back to the task at hand, and he wheeled the lawnmower back to the neighbor's garage, closing the door from outside. He knocked on the door and after a brief exchange, left with two five dollar bills and an appointment for the next week. He hurried back down the street to his house to shower, and found himself looking forward to seeing Chelle later.

The last ride to Tinker's had been with the group, and Bill hadn't been paying attention to time, but now, solo, it seemed to take longer. After a quick sandwich his mother insisted on, he had started later than he'd liked, nearly forgetting his towel and swimming trunks.

Within an hour he had arrived at the park, and rode his bike up the winding cobble road from the street to the parking lot, finding it nearly full of cars. He found an available slot at the bicycle rack, and surveyed the scene.

Ahead were a dozen picnic benches occupied with families. Nearby their kids played with squirt guns and water balloons and the smoke from numerous barbecue grills hung in the air.

Beyond was the minimal 'beach', a ten-foot wide strand of sand dotted with towels and teenage sunbathers that skirted a small portion of the irregularly-shaped lake. Children splashed in the shallows and teens and adults swam further out towards the buoy line, which demarcated the swimming portion of the lake.

The remainder of the lake was surrounded by forest with the exception of a trail that circled the shore, and at the most distant portion were several individuals fishing, though far enough to remain safe for the swimmers. During his prior visit he'd seen small fish and found it unusual sharing the water with wildlife, having only been in public pools. Still, the water was clearer that the backyard swimming pool of algae.

Scanning the crowds, he didn't see Chelle or Gloria anywhere, until he heard his name shouted from the lake. Bill didn't recognize her at first with her hair wet, but it was clearly Chelle waving, beckoning him to join her group in the deep end. He held up his trunks and made a quick motion to the restrooms, indicating he would join them as soon as he changed.

Finding an open stall, he traded his outfit for trunks, and exiting the structure, located a spot in the sand to stow his towel, clothes and shoes. He waded into the water, swimming over to the deep portion, greeting Chelle, Gloria and the rest of their gathering.

Time flew as the group raced, tossed a Frisbee, played underwater tag and chased each other around. Chelle seemed happy to see Bill, though they didn't converse much with all of the activity, until they took a brief break.

Heading to the beach for their towels, the sun hadn't quite set as the park attendees began to thin and families cleaned up and packed their cars. There were only a few people still swimming, but plenty of kids were still making a ruckus playing nearby. Still quite balmy out, they didn't need their towels much, and Bill and Chelle finally had a chance to catch up about their respective summers.

As Bill conversed with Chelle, he thought it might be rude to Gloria to show interest in her friend, but more importantly, would Chelle even like him back, and if he did let her know, would it screw up their friendship? He wondered how it had gotten so complicated as he noticed Chelle's blonde hair beginning to curl as it dried out. He subtly shook his head.

One of their group had brought a cooler and passed around cans of soda, and it was decided they would get a little more swimming in before dark. As it was, they weren't going anywhere until their ride came to pick them up, anyway.

As twilight took hold and the park attendees further dwindled, the faintest mist began to lift from the surface of the lake, its surface much calmer now as they waded between the shallows and deep end. Some of their group had returned to the beach leaving Bill, Chelle, Gloria, and one of her cousins in the water, which now seemed a more comfortable temperature than the evening air.

Bill noticed the first of several evening stars, pointing them out to Chelle. He also noticed the last of the cars leaving and the park now quiet except for their group. He was happy to be spending time with Chelle, and trying not to worry about mucking up their friendship.

Soon a car sped into the parking lot honking its horn, and Gloria called out that it was her brother having come to pick them up, as she and her cousin headed for the shore. Chelle asked him if he wanted to ride back with them, but he mentioned his bike which likely wouldn't fit.

Chelle said goodbye and surprised him, giving him a hug and kiss on the cheek before pushing for the shallows. Elated but stunned, Bill found himself grinning, realizing she actually liked him back. Rather than risk messing up what was a perfect parting, he decided to wait briefly before exiting the water.

He heard them pack into the car and saw their tail lights fade, wondering when he might see her again. The park grew quiet except for a steady chorus of crickets and frogs, and though there was only a small light near the restrooms busy with moths, Bill's eyes soon adjusted to the dark as he began wading for the shore.

Where a dark figure stood.

He stopped and squinted, unsure if he was just seeing a tree or some other object, and he began to slowly wade laterally, along the shore away from it. Glancing back after some distance, he couldn't tell if it was still there or not, so he waited, scanning the beach. Near the restroom, he thought he saw something, but staring at the light messed up his nighttime vision. He wondered if it was some older teenage kids who stuck around to mess with him.

He listened and waited, thought briefly about swimming to the other side of the lake to get out, then settled on wading further out to get away from the light. Sure enough, there was something dark, large and motionless on the sand where there was nothing before, he was almost sure.

Sure enough to begin to be spooked.

He decided to swim beyond the buoys to the other side of the lake, remembering what one of their group had said about it being

REALLY deep. Luckily he was a decent swimmer, his parents having taken him for lessons years earlier. He dove under and swam beneath the surface as far as he could before coming up for a breath. He was almost a third of the way across and looked back at the beach, but the surface mists obscured the shore.

He submerged once more, and kicked his legs and paddled until coming up again. He was only about ten yards from the other side, and could make out the silhouettes of the trees against the night sky. He took a breath, and right before going under to continue, he saw something dark move along the trail.

He re-emerged and treaded water, reevaluating his destination. There was a distinct form ahead. Submerging, he spun underwater and headed back for the buoy line.

Emerging close to the buoy line he evaluated his options, felt the onset of a cramp in his left leg, and treaded water. He'd now been in the water for quite some time, and knew he wouldn't be able to stay in the deep portion forever. Paddling over, he slipped under the buoy line and held on. It wouldn't support his weight completely, but it helped enough to rub his thigh with his free hand.

Peering through the lessening mist he was unable to see anything on the beach, and wondered if he could make it to the sand and to his bike quick enough to outrun... whatever. There was the farthest point of the lake as a possible exit, where the fishermen were, but with his leg cramping, he ruled that out.

He caught a tiny glint of light beyond the beach, farthest from the restrooms, and focused on the area. He recalled a science class lesson about structures in the eye called rods and cones, remembering one had better low light vision when not looking directly at something, so he trained his eyes adjacent to where he had seen the flash.

It was one of the shapes, and it was massive. Again the glint—this time a pair. High up on the figure, he realized they were wet reflections from the restroom light, from the eyes of something watching him. He knew it couldn't be the same one from the other side of the lake, there was more than one, and one was already one too many. This was not good.

He wondered how long he could stay in the water. He wasn't yet cold, but the temperature was dropping. Though he knew he was… trapped, he did have the buoy line to stay afloat, his leg cramp appeared to have subsided, and luckily so far, whatever was on shore was staying on shore.

Then came the SPLASH! Distant, from the fishermen's side of the lake, but a splash nonetheless. Bill froze, beginning to feel the chill, and strained to see the source of the noise..

A brief flash of light flared and he saw tops of trees illuminate around one side of the lake. He thought lightning, but there were no clouds in the sky, only stars. The flicker grew steady, and he heard the growing drone of an engine. Seconds later came the crunch of gravel compacting and bright floodlights nearly blinded him. He heard a car door open and close and a voice shout:

"You there! Come on out of the water! Park's closed!"

He immediately swam for the shore, his eyes adjusting to the light, and once in the shallows, was happy to feel the bottom beneath his feet. He looked for the shapes, but they were nowhere to be seen, and he quickly made way for his towel and clothes, scooping them up and hurrying up to the car.

"What are you doing out here at night? I have to lock up the gate. Get in, I'll give you a lift," offered the driver, who Bill saw wearing a duty belt and radio, motioning over to the passenger side of his cruiser.

Bill quickly walked over to the vehicle, the police light bar no longer obscured by the floodlights. He had never been in a police car, but welcomed the opportunity. This was the literal cavalry, and he thanked the stars above for its arrival.

He opened the side door, and saw the officer scanning around with his flashlight. Bill quickly got in and pulled the door shut, but his towel caught in the door's mechanism, and the door refused to latch properly. Bill remembered his bike as the officer opened the driver side door.

"My bike is still here, should I—" Bill excitedly remarked, though in the interest of leaving, he was ready to abandon it.

"Stay here, I'll put it in the trunk," the officer quickly replied. Bill was about to protest, but before he could begin explaining about 'strange beings around the lake', the officer had closed his door.

Bill brushed sand from his feet and pulled on his sneakers, as he heard the officer open the trunk. He tugged at his towel and pulled the door handle in an attempt to free it, before he heard the driver's side door open.

"Sorry, my towel's stu—" Bill saw light out the passenger window. The officer was walking away towards the bike rack with his flashlight.

The hair stood up on the back of Bill's neck. If the officer didn't open the door...

Something else had. He was too terrified to turn and see, afraid of what might be STARING back at him.

The flashlight blinded and startled him. "Are you here with anyone else?" he heard the officer call from a few yards away, and before Bill could reply, the light swung away to the restroom. He saw the officer draw his pistol, and approach the stalls.

Trembling, Bill slowly mustered the will to glance behind to the open driver's door.

Nothing.

"Who's out there?!" He heard the distant officer shout. Bill quickly pulled on his shirt, keeping a sharp eye on the open door, as he then felt the car shudder.

Something had bumped it from behind.

He heard the crunch of gravel as the car inched forward towards the beach and stopped.

He quickly discarded the idea of staying put, and he tugged on his door handle once more in vain. There was clearly something outside, but remaining in the car wouldn't do much good if it was pushed into the water ahead. He was about to shout for the officer, as the car shuddered forth once more.

He had to act. He searched for a weapon, but found the console and seat bare and the glove box locked. Leaving his towel behind he crawled over to the driver seat and quickly peered out to the rear. The gravel behind lit up red, and he realized his feet had tapped the brakes. He didn't know how to drive a car, but knew keys were a necessity, and the officer had taken them with him.

Tapping the brake once more, he illuminated the rear, and unable to see anything, crept from the car. Quickly leaving the glow of the dome light, he huddled near the base of a tree. A clatter of wood knocking issued from the restroom building, though Bill could see nothing. The rear of the car and parking lot also appeared clear, and he spotted the outline of his bike nearby.

When the shooting started, he ran for his bike. When the screaming started, he frantically ran with it at length before leaping on and pedalling in the dark to the road and ultimately, back to his home.

Police were summoned, and eventually investigated the park, but found nothing suspicious. Additionally, no local police or park rangers were reported missing.

Complaints of an oil sheen years later prompted a temporary lake closure, until dredgers pulled a car from the lake. The vehicle had been made to look like a patrol car and belonged to an individual of interest in several missing person investigations.

A body was never recovered.

1979

1979 was the year Mitch got scared. He'd always had an interest in monster movies, but everything he saw on TV consisted of Godzilla, Bigfoot or Vincent Price movies, and those didn't scare him one bit. He'd seen plenty of fright films thanks to the regular Friday night Hoolihan and Big Chuck show, as well as from the Superhost twin feature the following day.

But he knew there was a world of even scarier movies out there that he wasn't yet allowed to see, being only ten years old. He pored over the newspaper ads for movies opening each week at the drive-ins, as regular theaters didn't book some of the more frightening options. The tiny graphic adverts and bold titles mystified him, and seeing the distinctive brand of the boxed letter 'R' for restricted signified something forbidden, that if seen, could really warp his mind.

At least that's what he was told, and he remembers believing it. After borrowing a box full of old Famous Monsters magazines from his friend Gary earlier that year, the light-hearted approach the magazine offered served to de-fang the subject considerably.

Still, some of the ads caught hold of his imagination, warning against 'opening the door' or 'going in the basement', and he wondered what a 'Phantasm' was. When he'd asked his father about the films, his father would usually make a joke about them before telling him to ask his mother for permission to watch, knowing the answer would be 'no' as long as they were rated 'R'.

Earlier that summer on a multi-screen drive-in visit with his folks he'd kept track of what was showing on the other distant screens. Later in the night he was able to watch portions of 'The Amityville Horror' from the back seat of the family car. But with the screen tiny and lacking sound, there was hardly any horror to be seen through that rear window.

So he kept track of movies that he wanted to see, and when hanging out with his friends would talk about titles such as 'Prophecy', 'Alien' and 'Halloween', in the hopes that they might have been able to see them. Many summer afternoons were filled with monster movie discussions, comic book trading and handheld electronic games, usually in the treehouse in his friend Damon's backyard.

Down the street from Mitch and nestled at the edge of his backyard in a small copse of trees, the tree fort had been built by Damon's father a few years prior. Only seven feet off the ground and with a ladder beneath providing floor access, the accommodations were cramped, the roof leaked, but the view was decent. The wooden shutters could be propped open, offering a view of a dozen backyards on one side, and a tall grass field that stretched hundreds of yards on the other.

Their sanctum had come under invasion as of late, with Damon's younger sister and her friends requesting access. When denied they would end up playing right outside, spoiling the seclusion, which led to arguments and ultimately the dreaded word — share. His sister had the first half of the day, and Damon got the latter.

It was their friend Todd who finally suggested they construct their own fort elsewhere, and soon Mitch, Gary, Damon and Todd began brainstorming locations for their new fort. After each other's backyards were ruled out, their next choice for secrecy lay in the woods beyond the fields.

Having some familiarity with the nearby woods, they set about exploring for a suitable location. After rejecting several candidate locations, they soon found a spot deeper in that had no obvious trails, was thick with ground foliage, and had plenty of tall straight trunks that could serve as foundations.

The plan was not to build a single structure housed in one tree, but to construct a base floor that spanned between three to four trees, like a house on stilts. Over the next few days they began scrounging for lumber, ultimately amassing a small pile, which with difficulty was trekked far out to their destination.

They'd nearly gotten in serious trouble when Todd suggested they gather leftovers from a local home construction site, waiting until the workers had left for lunch. As the group was attempting to make off with several sheets of plywood, the workers returned immediately, catching them in the act and chasing them off. Wisely, they did not return.

Still, they had enough to begin constructing the base platform, and after some hammer practice and many bent nails, had makeshift ladders up several adjacent trunks. Using the longest two by fours they secured a triangular base nearly twelve feet off the forest floor. The remainder of their lumber allowed them to fill in the platform with a hodgepodge floor, followed of course, by a requisite weight test.

With more than a little apprehension they each climbed onto the platform. Damon and Todd first stepped over to take hold of two of the supporting trunks, followed by Todd who stepped to the middle as Mitch came up last. The boards creaked beneath their feet, but held their weight. Without a handhold, Todd was the first to mention the need for rails.

The group acknowledged their handiwork and how large the platform looked from below, but now from above, they found the triangular floor plan lacking in size. With an eye line height of seventeen feet off the forest floor, Gary joked they may have built the fort too high.

Collecting their tools below the treehouse, they noted how conspicuous the platform was above, blotting out the daylight and casting a pool of shade below. This late in the day the emphasis of shadows in the woods was not unusual, though the contrast was evident as they walked out into the brighter fields.

Stopping to climb up into the fort in Damon's backyard, they compared how much higher and larger their new fort was, even if it was lacking walls, windows, and a roof... basically all the necessary elements to complete their distant project.

Until scrounging up more materials they knew their project was on hold, which served to deflate the day's enthusiasm.

They were about to part on that sentiment when Damon blurted, "Mitch, I almost forgot, last weekend, I saw THE EXORCIST!"

Mitch was all ears, and though Todd had to depart for supper, he and Gary wanted to hear all about it, though his account was halted before sharing. Damon's older sister Cheryl summoned him with a shout for dinner, delaying the story until they could regroup after their respective dinners.

It was half past eight when Mitch and the others returned to Damon's garage, whose parents had left for the evening. From atop the riding mower, Damon related having gone to a drive-in the previous Saturday with older cousins, hiding in the back of a station wagon to catch a double feature of THE OMEN and THE EXORCIST. Though the two movies had been out for many years, Mitch knew they still played heavily at late-night drive-ins.

As Damon worked his way through the most shocking parts of THE OMEN and the discussion that followed, they were interrupted by the throaty exhaust and headlights of a car pulling into the driveway. Loud guitar music blared for several seconds before quieting. The car door opened and closed, and the tall driver paused briefly in their light, sporting a denim jacket and long hair, nodding briefly to the group.

"Hey Damon," he greeted before heading around the side to the front door entrance.

Damon had uttered a "hey," in return and after they heard the squeak of the screen door opening and closing, he explained that he was his sister Cheryl's boyfriend Rory, and though he looked much older, was attending in a vocational school nearby.

Damon motioned them all close as he shared in a hushed whisper, "I think he was held back."

Fifteen minutes later Damon's recollection of THE EXORCIST left Mitch somewhat disappointed, and he began to suspect that Damon either fell asleep while viewing the film or was making the story up, as it made little sense. The screen door opened again and Rory and Cheryl walked past the garage, where Damon's sister asked him to keep an eye on their younger sister while she was out.

Damon knew she was technically charged with babysitting their younger sister while their parents were out, and that it was up to him to keep quiet about it. "What's in it for me? " he quizzed her.

Before she could get riled up, Rory spoke, "That wasn't THE EXORCIST you saw, you described the sequel, THE EXORCIST 2 THE HERETIC."

"How do you—" Cheryl interrupted herself, knowing Rory's explanation had diverted her brother's attention.

"I've seen it, and have a friend who works at a theater. He says they leave off the full title so people think it's the original, and they make more money, even after refunds," Rory explained.

"Tell us about the Exorcist!" Mitch blurted out, barely able to contain his enthusiasm, with Damon, Gary and Todd echoing his sentiment.

Rory exchanged glances with Cheryl and pulled a wooden crate from the garage to sit on. "Alright. I'll tell you about the movie, and if Damon can keep a secret, I'll do one better. I'll tell ya a story... A scary *true* story."

Even with his friends urging, Damon quickly relented, and Cheryl briefly went inside, returning with canned RC colas to further sweeten the bribe. They listened as Rory told the highlights from the film, but more what the theatre crowd reception had been like when he'd seen it years prior. Rory's firsthand account of the film made him more intent on seeing it than before.

"Cheryl said you were building a treehouse out in the woods," Rory took a long drink from his can, and then stared at each of the four boys, who variously nodded and confirmed his statement.

"Well, I used to build tree forts when I was your age too. Maybe eight, nine miles that way on the other side of the forest is the neighborhood I grew up in. Back then the forest stretched for miles, this whole neighborhood hadn't yet been put in," He motioned at the surrounding houses.

"Our neighborhood was relatively new then too, where my friends and I lived, except for an older house at the far end of our street. There was a boy that lived there, older than us, named Herschel, and he was a little strange. He'd either dropped out or been kicked out of school. Who knows what he did with his time.

"We used to run around in the woods, and every now and then we'd come across these big holes, sometimes half dug fire pits, sometimes partially covered over with boards, not far from this kid's house. We followed him one day as he left his house, walked into the woods and he disappeared into the ground," Rory whistled and made a downward motion with his hand.

"We stayed for awhile, but he didn't come out until much later. And when we were sure he was gone we looked in the hole. He'd pretty much dug small tunnels and had a room with a sleeping bag, candles, wood planks, everything," Rory continued.

"What was he doing down there?" Mitch asked, and Rory just shrugged.

"We were looking for a place to build our forts, and decided to do it far away from this kid, so we went a completely different direction in the woods. Every now and then we'd find these burned up trees but didn't think nothing of it, and eventually built a pretty cool fort up in this tree. Well, when we came back the next day, the thing had been torched; someone had set it on fire.

"Anyway, the next summer my folks split up and I went to live with my mom up near the lake. I heard later that my friends had built another tree house later that summer, and on a dare, they'd camped out in it overnight.

"Middle of the night, they wake up just in time to jump out of the tree house before the whole thing went up in flames. As it was, one shattered an ankle, another broke an arm and they all got burned pretty bad," Rory took a sip from his can.

"There was an investigation, and my friends told of the fire pits out near Herschel's house, and they found his underground hideouts, supposedly with books on the occult. They said he was a firebug, a pyromaniac, and he got sent away, which was the last I'd heard of it... until recently.

"Remember that barn out on Frost Road that burned down last summer? I heard Herschel had been released not long before, and that no one has seen him since," Rory concluded.

Before Rory and Cheryl left, he gave them a final warning. "Beware... if you go out in those woods, watch out for fires, and watch out for Herschel... he's still out there."

After moving to the family room for more cola and chips, Gary wondered to the group. "Do you think any of that is true... Do you really think that happened?"

"Maybe. But he did hear about us talking about scary movies, so he might have just made it up to scare us..." Mitch replied with a mouthful of chips, confident that the story hadn't scared him.

"Yeah... But he did give me an idea about more wood for the fort," Damon swallowed the last of his cola and let out a huge burp.

It was a few days later before they were all able to regroup, when Damon soon led them to the remains of the burned out barn along Frost road. Most of the decrepit structure had been destroyed, but the local volunteer fire department had showed up before the flames could consume it entirely.

Amidst the blackened and sooty debris they were able to locate several usable planks, as well as a nearby woodpile that had been untouched by the fire, overgrown with weeds and tall grasses. It appeared to be old wood siding from a house, and after removing the top rotted layers they were able to salvage a quantity of thin grey planks.

It took several arduous trips with a wheelbarrow to relocate the majority of the woodpile to their fort site, and by the end of the week had framed walls and a crude roof on their three-sided fort. A simple plywood door hinged open as their entry way, and small rectangular cutouts served as windows on each side of the structure.

It was late afternoon as the four stood in their finished tree house, when Damon shushed the group repeatedly, crouching in the fort. "Did you hear that?" He whispered.

First Mitch, then Todd and Gary played along, crouching down similarly. As seconds ticked by they scrutinized Mitch's face, and soon their grins began to fade.

"What did you hear?" Todd whispered to Mitch.

"I swear... I heard... a LIGHTER!" Damon cracked up, and was met with groans and curse words from the remaining three. "Man, I had you guys going... but seriously, we should stay here - TONIGHT!"

"Are you kidding?" Todd asked incredulously.

"Sure we can stand, but there's not enough room for the four of us to lay down in here..." Gary explained, laying flat on the floor.

"Besides, the mosquitoes will eat us up if we don't cover the windows..." Mitch contributed as the trio continued with additional excuses.

Finally Damon countered, "Alright, ya bunch of scaredy cats, you don't really believe that story, do ya? — That's all it was, a story to scare us. We built this thing, we gotta use it. Let's say Saturday night. That'll give us a few days to get permission, cover the windows, bring a bunch of flashlights, BB guns, the ones with the pellets... and we don't have to make it a dare."

By late Saturday afternoon Mitch had told his parents that they were sleeping over at Damon's, with Todd and Gary employing similar cover stories. Though they hadn't been back to the tree house since to to cover the windows, Todd had gotten hold of a big can of insect repellant, and they geared up.

An hour later they had trekked to the site of their fort, and Todd and Gary lugged their sleeping bags and other gear up into the fort while Mitch helped Damon set up an alarm. Beyond the area they had trampled during construction, they began stringing fishing line between trees at knee height in a wide circle around their fort.

After nearly stepping on a nail, Mitch found a lot of unused planks underneath the Mayapples and fern floor cover, pointing out to Damon they probably still had enough wood left over to build a second story. Once their trip wire was complete, they hung empty cola cans at regular intervals, where anyone walking into the invisible line would alert them, and draw fire from their pellet guns.

After an additional dousing of chemical repellant, the four climbed into their accommodations complaining of the odor. Over Marathon bars they negotiated for sleeping bag space in the tight quarters as daylight faded…

Mitch sat up with a jolt, realized he had nodded off, and that a noise had woken him. In the dim glow of the lantern he could see the others had fallen asleep as well, and he shook at Todd and Damon, waking them.

He then heard the cans clank together, rattling several times. Gary was now awake, and they traded wide eyed glances as they reached for their flashlights, noticing the sky still in twilight.

"What is it?" Gary whispered, as Damon cocked his pellet gun. They heard the cans rattle once more at length.

"Who else knows we're out here?" Todd whispered as Damon peered over the edge of the cutout window.

"No one," Damon replied.

"GET ON OUT OF THERE RIGHT NOW, THAT IS NOT YOUR TREE HOUSE!" A male voice shouted from the forest shadows.

"What do you see?" hissed Gary frantically, as Mitch peaked over the edge, seeing nothing.

"I knew this was a bad idea," trembled Todd as Mitch fumbled in the dark for his BB gun.

"I SAID GET OUT NOW. I'LL GIVE YOU THE COUNT OF THREE!"

Damon took a shot in the dark towards the sound of the voice, ducking down to pump the rifle again, as they heard a familiar click and low whoosh sound from outside. Damon paused momentarily and peeked over the edge briefly.

"ONE!"

"It's a torch! I can't see him!" Damon stammered, as the nearby orange glow lit up the interior of the fort.

"TWO!"

"What do we do?! Todd whimpered, as Mitch realized he was not only scared but trembling, that Gary was petrified, and Damon was peering over the edge with his pellet gun, wide eyed.

"THREE!"

"OKAY!!!" Mitch shouted, his voice shaking. "WE'RE COMING OUT NOW!" He pushed Todd to the door, who struggled to get it open, before Damon pushed him aside to kick the door open. Todd scrambled out to the ladder, followed by Gary who Damon shoved out. The moments Mitch waited for his turn to exit couldn't come soon enough, and he briefly considered leaping from a window as the last moments of daylight faded.

"HURRY!! THAT IS NOT YOUR HOUSE!"

As Mitch finally reached the ladder his shirt snagged on the door, which slammed into him. He felt his shirt rip as he struggled to tear free of the door, causing him to fumble his grip and footing, before falling-

As he landed on his back with a resounding THUD! he heard his friends running off. With the wind knocked out and struggling to breathe saw the flaming bottle sail into the window of the fort above.

With a whoosh and a shriek he saw flames shoot from the three open windows, and the supporting trees began to twist...

He felt hands grab under his arms and drag him into the brush as the noises from the tree house grew louder and stranger, and from beneath the cover of Mayapple leaves saw the fort engulfed with flame, and writhing...

A moment later he realized he was underground and in a tunnel, with tiny shards of light from the fire above dancing through the darkness. He was not alone in the tunnel, and as his eyes adjusted he saw a scraggly face staring at the trapdoor above.

The sounds of splintering, CRACKING and ROAR of the fire could be heard above as the man's eyes caught Mitch's. He held his finger to his lips for silence, as thunderous footfalls STOMPED overhead, shaking the tunnel around them as something MASSIVE and hungry searched for them above.

The light and heat in the tunnel grew as the inferno raged above them, until Mitch could heard a horrible MEWLING over the roar, when the light finally faded as THUMPS rapidly retreated further into the forest.

"I didn't think you'd make it. It feeds after sunset," The scruffy man broke the silence, at last switching on a penlight. "It must have taken the place of your house last night. Come on, follow me…"

"Did—Did you kill it?" Mitch gulped.

"For now," said Herschel.

TEUFEL

Brett's savings had been nearly wiped out, victim to the latest automotive repair bill, and his car was still in the shop. He'd worked the three and a half months of summer at Geauga Lake Amusement park, and banked almost every paycheck. After the season had ended, he hadn't taken a new job, planning to coast out the final year of high school on his summer earnings.

His engine had other plans however, and after an emergency tow and ride from his father, found he'd be without the Monte Carlo for the next week, while the garage ordered necessary replacement parts. He knew he'd need to pick up a part time job soon, but that it'd have to wait until he got his car back. Luckily his friend Duane was around for rides in the meantime; avoiding the use of the school bus, a mode of transportation he'd hoped was in his past.

It was a Friday after school and they'd headed over to a closed mini-golf location Duane still had the keys to, having closed the place up for the season the previous weekend. Picking putters and a handful of primary colored golf balls, they teed up among the miniature buildings.

"Don't you need to return the keys yet?" Brett swung his putter, noting the accumulation of dead leaves now on the course. It had only been two weeks since they were last here, but autumn had really changed the feel of the place. That and the lack of customers.

"Nah, they don't care. They went out of town before the season ended, asked me to keep an eye on the place. I think they were just shocked I didn't rip 'em off over the summer," Duane laughed and swung his club. The ball sailed past Brett's, stopping just short of the hole. "Sucks about your car," he added, as several amber and gold maple leaves fluttered onto the course.

They were halfway through the course when another car pulled into the gravel lot nearby, and they were soon joined by their friend Drew and his girlfriend Sandy. "What brings you to our neck of the woods, beside the wonderful world of putt-putt?" Duane greeted the approaching couple.

"Were headed over to Chapel Hill to catch a movie, saw your car here," Drew explained, before Sandy interrupted him.

"Hudson Haunted House, tomorrow night, you two are going, right? There's going to be a group of us and you should go!" she said.

Brett wondered if his wallet could bear the cost of admission. Suddenly every minor expense loomed large after his recent financial hit, and it probably made sense to stop all spending altogether... then he heard Duane confirm his attendance.

"Brett? What about you? I've got a friend I'd like you to meet. She'll be there and she's pretty cute, I think I have a picture. I told her you'd be there," Sandy explained, fishing through her purse.

"Hey, what about me, am I chopped liver?" Duane swung his club at a pile of leaves, scattering them near a miniature wooden church.

"I doubt you two would get along, but I might have someone in mind for you Duane." She pulled a photo from a billfold in her purse and handed it to Brett. "Her name's Robin," she added. Sandy hadn't lied. The red-haired girl was pretty.

By six o'clock the next day Duane had picked Brett up, and after grabbing a burger they headed over towards the annual haunted attraction. Turning onto Barlow road, they joined the line of cars queued for parking, and attendants with flashlights eventually guided them to overflow grass parking far in the back.

After loitering in the parking lot for several minutes, they made their way to the ticket booth and bought admission, before searching the backed-up line of patrons for Sandy and Drew. Though floodlights illuminated the area, the crowd revealed no familiar faces. Duane had gone looking for a restroom when Brett heard his name from the parking lot.

Weaving through parked cars, Sandy led a group of four other girls followed by Drew, who broke off as a group before he could greet them, leaving Drew with Brett. "Finally some quiet. Want a smoke?" Drew kidded as he lit up a cigarette. Brett declined and they chatted about his car until Duane returned, who complained about the line at the urinal until Drew gave him a cigarette.

When the girls returned, Sandy introduced Robin to Brett, and another girl to Duane, and the group took a place in line. "I think I saw you renting videos over the summer," Robin had to repeat over the crowd, following some nervous small talk between the two. "But you were with someone—what was her name," she teased, referring to a girl Brett dated briefly.

"Videos? Oh yeah, that's over. It was mutual," he quickly clarified and made a mental note to apply for a job at the video store.

The two seemed to hit it off over the next hour as they waited in line, and when their turn finally came to enter the attraction, she clutched his arm in advance. He didn't mind she chose him as her human shield over the group safety afforded by her friends, though by the end several of the other girls were huddled directly behind him and Robin.

"You were pretty tough in there, I don't think you screamed at all," Brett laughed as they exited.

"Piece of cake… actually my eyes were closed for most of it!" Robin confessed with a shudder, as they followed the group over to a nearby refreshment stand.

Within minutes they were eating donuts and drinking cups of coffee and hot chocolate, their breath visible as they mocked each other's reactions while inside the maze.

Brett felt a tap on his shoulder while taking a sip. "Brett?" asked an unexpected yet familiar male voice, and Brett turned to the source. "I thought that was you!" He recognized Shea, a former coworker from Geauga Lake who'd somehow escaped being fired on more than one occasion. Shea was with a group of his friends, and a rough introduction was made between the two groups. Halfway through a work story, Shea's girlfriend tugged at his varsity jacket and he got the hint, quickly wrapping up his story.

"Hey, what are you doing later? We are talking about heading out to check out something really spooky," a collective groan issued from Shea's group, and he dismissed them as he continued his story. "Come on, it's not like we're going out looking for Melonheads! These guys don't want to go at night. Remember I told you my dad works for the park? Someone died and donated a bunch of old maps from the twenties, and the oldest references something called—get this—'Teufels Krypta.'"

By now, Shea's tale had gotten the group's full attention, and they reacted with jeers at the name. "For real, as in crypt?" exclaimed Sandy, and the girls with Shea responded with similar incredulity.

"Where is this place?" Drew asked, and Sandy playfully hit his arm.

"It's pretty much a left and straight shot down Barlow Road about five miles to the ledges trailhead parking area. You know where Ice Box cave is? It's not even that far, maybe a few hundred feet from the parking lot. If you guys go, then they might go!" Shea motioned to his group.

Brett glanced over at Duane and then to Robin, who sipped her cocoa. Having just met her he wasn't sure how she'd react to whether he'd participate or not, but fortunately the issue was out of his hands anyway, what with Duane having driven.

"Yeah, let's check it out!" Duane exclaimed, eager to impress at least one of Sandy's friends. When Drew echoed the sentiment, Brett knew declining was no longer an option. Robin looked at him for an answer and he quickly explained that Duane had driven, and that his car was in the shop.

"You know 'Teufel' is German for the devil, right?" Robin informed the group.

"That's what's so cool, and makes it so much more fun than this!" Shea motioned at the attraction and finished with mock maniacal laughter. "This is the season, after all!" A collective agreement was reached to follow Shea's car and they dispersed to locate their parked vehicles.

"Hey, if you don't want to go, maybe we could wait here for them to return?" Brett suggested to Robin before they split.

"What, and have you think I'm afraid?" She chuckled briefly. "But I think I'm going to ride with you, if that's all right!"

Another of Robin's friends joined them, and within minutes the four of them followed Shea's car from the parking lot onto Barlow road, followed by Drew's car. "That makes twelve of us. I think the most we have to worry about is making too much noise and getting chased out by the cops, assuming they haven't chained up the parking lot already," Duane calmly stated, as he fiddled with the radio station selector.

"Where do you know him—that guy—from?" Robin leaned across the backseat, pointing to the car ahead of them.

"Shea? We worked together over the summer—sort of together. He worked in one of the barker stands near mine. He's a goofball and I think his family's loaded, but he's all right. Threw a massive party when his folks were out of town, supposedly had over twenty kegs, or so I heard. I had to work," he explained. "How did you know that word, 'Teufel'?" Brett asked Robin.

"My grandmother is German, I spent a lot of summers with her," she replied.

Traffic thinned out as they entered the park boundaries, and their three cars drove onto the gravel drive that led to the empty parking lot. Following Shea's lead, they parked close to the trailhead. There was a flurry of excitement as they exited their vehicles, remarking at the growing chill and complete lack of light sources. Duane popped open his trunk and found a pair of flashlights, while Brett reached for several red stick road flares. Drew, Sandy and her friends soon joined them with another flashlight, while Shea shined what appeared to be a heavy duty lantern flashlight at the group.

"How far in is this place?" Sandy echoed her friends' sentiments.

"Literally, right around the curve in the trail. We'll be there in like two, three minutes tops. But everyone, stay on the trail. There are a lot of rocks and uneven ground… and stick together! Everybody good?" Shea acknowledged their collective response, and with his

150

group in tow, led them down the trail.

Brett handed his flashlight to Robin, who held onto his jacket with her other hand. Duane and the rest of the girls were closely followed by Sandy and Drew, who Brett noticed had brought a tire iron. He kept a crowbar in his own car, but little good it did him now.

The various light sources and general rowdiness of the group kept the overall atmosphere light as they shuffled through the layer of leaves blanketing the trail. The trees still held onto enough of their canopy to blot out the stars, and a faint breeze whispered through the branches above.

"I thought you said not to leave the trail," came a voice near the front.

"It's right up here!" Shea proclaimed, stepping up onto a series of massive shelf-like rocks. A colossal slab behind him displayed his silhouette as the various flashlights illuminated him. "This is it! The Teufels Krypta!" he announced, under lighting his face with his lantern.

As the group gathered round, Brett took the opportunity to light one of his road flares, removing and striking the cap. First sparks, then a short red flame and smoke issued forth from the flare, and the group reacted to the new light source. "Brett, can you bring that here for a moment?" Shea requested, referring to the flare. Brett stepped forward and passed the flare to Shea.

"The old maps highlighted this location, though it doesn't seem to be on any subsequent or modern maps, so it's either been forgotten, or intentionally omitted from more recent maps," Brett noticed Shea was using the same voice he used over the summer, selling the 'carnival-like' attraction aspect.

Shea took a few steps to his right, and as the group watched, he held the flare out at arm's length briefly, then dropped it. They were surprised to see the light vanish, before a clatter echoed moments later. Shea turned off his flashlight and a faint flickering red glow came from below, highlighted by dissipating smoke. "Step right up, and have a look!" he invited the group.

They variously took turns peeking over the edge into a small rectangular hole, and when Brett and Robin stepped up for their glance; Brett spotted the flare resting on a rock floor a dozen feet below. The shaft was too narrow for any adult to fit through and climb down, as was his first inclination after seeing what might have been a passageway at the bottom. He was curious, if not a little disappointed. "So is that it?"

"Actually, from the documents that were donated, back at the start of the last century everyone was obsessed with spirits," Shea explained.

Robin interjected. "You mean spiritualism?"

"Exactly, and people around here used to have séances at this location, with mediums and talking boards, with the tradition of making declarations of something very important into the hole." Shea paused for dramatic effect, the attention of the group now focused on his tale.

"Important? Like what?" Sandy broke the silence.

"It was a kind of dare, where first you would announce to the hole your name, and then whether you were a brave soul, or had fear in your heart," Shea explained matter-of-factly, as the glow from the hole faded, the flare sputtering out.

"Who wants to go first? Anyone... all right, I'll go first. My name is Shea and I am not afraid," he announced into the hole. His friends laughed, and then slowly followed his example, with similar reactions.

Duane was the first of their group to join in. "This is silly. I am not afraid, and oh yeah, my name is Duane," he declared into the hole while grinning back at Robin's friend.

Drew and Sandy approached with hesitation and they started to speak simultaneously. "My name is Drew and I'm not—" he stopped as Sandy paused after stating her name, but followed with "and I'm a little scared," she laughed it off, prompting Drew to add: "I change my answer, I am scared too," he joked, which was met with a few jeers from the group. The remaining girls paused and focused on Robin, whereby Brett realized it was their turn. He turned to offer her a hand to step towards the hole.

"Yeah, I'm not doing that," Robin declared, shaking her head. "You can, but I'm not," she was serious and the tone of the group shifted. Brett knew participating at this point would be a bad idea, as it certainly wasn't going to impress Robin.

"What about you, Brett? Are you afraid?" Shea asked.

"I… I think we oughta start heading back," Brett replied.

"All right, it would appear Brett and his gal would fall into the 'afraid' category," Shea attempted to conclude with a 'sportscaster's' voice, but led by Brett and Robin, the group began returning towards the trail and parking lot.

After some driving arrangements, Duane and Brett drove Robin and her friend home, following an awkward departure from the park, while Duane played music to lighten the mood. Brett was pretty sure things with Robin were a bust until she gave him her number before she left.

Though he had no idea how soon he should call, he dialed immediately after Duane dropped him off. "Sorry if I ruined your evening, but I don't like to mess around with things like that," she explained, and they talked for the next hour before making plans for the following weekend, when his car would hopefully be out of the shop.

Fulfilling a promise to his parents made several days prior; Brett spent most of Sunday afternoon raking leaves in their yard. The front yard took the better part of an hour, and after bagging the multi-colored piles, he'd worked up a sweat in spite of the chill in the air. As the cold began to catch up to him, he went inside to don a plaid over shirt, and noticed his parents had gone out.

He'd finished about half of the backyard when a breeze began to pick up, blowing more leaves into the yard from up the street. He quickly went to retrieve more bags to contain the existing piles, and returned to find the back yard a mess again, a small dervish of leaves scattering his handiwork. "One step forward, two steps back," he muttered and began raking again, accompanied by the rising hiss of leaves yet to fall.

By Friday night his car was ready, and his father took him to pick it up after he came home from work. He let Duane know he'd no longer need a ride, and he was able to pick Robin up on Saturday night, when they went to buy pumpkins from a seasonal farm. Situated next to an orchard and run as a business, bales of hay, bundles of Indian corn, and crude scarecrows adorned the grounds.

Pumpkins could be purchased from bins nearby or selected from an adjacent field that also hosted a tall corn maze—to which tickets could be purchased from the refreshment building, where Brett and Robin waited in line to purchase tall mugs of fresh-pressed cider.

Behind them in line was a group of teenage girls from a neighboring school district, as evidenced by their band jacket colors. Brett and Robin listened in silent amusement to the boisterous group as they edged closer to the counter—it was clear they were buying tickets for the maze and were daring each other to attempt it solo, and how scary that might be.

Their turn finally came at the counter, and Brett was mid-order when he overheard one of the girls gasp, "Oh my gosh, have you heard of the Devil's Grave?"

Robin immediately met his gaze, clearly as surprised to hear mention as was he, and the woman at the counter had to repeat, "Can I help you?" to the startled pair.

By Tuesday the following week, the pair noticed students at their school were talking about a 'Demon's Grave', and on Thursday, Brett's parents read a story in the local newspaper of a 'Haunted Local Park', and were curious to know if Brett had heard about it.

As his father read it aloud, the article detailed numerous acts of vandalism including graffiti, splattered red paint, burning debris, and fireworks that warranted multiple visits from the fire department, concluding that park officials would be monitoring and turning mischief makers away, now numbering in the scores each night. Brett told them he hadn't heard of it.

Following school on Friday night, Brett phoned Robin to let her know he'd be running a bit late to pick her up. She asked if he'd called earlier and hung up, which he hadn't. When Brett finally arrived, Robin mentioned that her phone had rang again after he'd called, with only static and a scratching noise. She thought it might be her friends playing a trick, but when she contacted them they relayed the news that Sandy had been hospitalized after several sick days out, wondering if she knew more.

This latest news only seemed to add to Robin's worries, of how word of the grave appeared to be spreading, of bad dreams she'd been having, and the ongoing prank calls. "What if all of this is related… to that place in the park?" she wondered aloud, prompting Brett to downplay the situation. "This time of year everyone is going to gravitate towards something scary, and just like the 'trick' in Trick 'r Treat, the phone calls are just another prank. At least they're not a heavy breather!" he joked, prompting her to smile and allaying some of her concerns.

But he now had a concern of his own, that he decided best not to share with Robin that evening: He hadn't seen Duane for the last few days. It was time to find out what Shea had gotten them involved in.

SATURDAY

The following morning his attempts to contact Shea proved to be difficult, as he didn't know his last name. He tried tracking down the few summer co-workers whose contact info he possessed that might also know Shea, leaving his callback info on several answering machines. Before he left that afternoon, Brett let his parents know he'd be going over to Robin's and to let him know if anyone called for him.

With her parents away for the evening at a costume party, Robin and Brett had decided to stay in for the evening. Robin had found an annual televised favorite about a ghost pumpkin to play in the background while they carved the pumpkins they'd purchased the week prior. Robin was pulling the guts out of her pumpkin when the phone rang, startling her.

"Have there been more calls today?" Brett asked her as she wiped pumpkin from her hands.

"A few," she replied, and he set down the carving knife.

"Let me get it," he offered.

"It might be my parents," she countered, answering the phone.

"Hello?" Brett could see from her furrowed brow it was another prank call, and prompting her for the handset, he put the phone to his ear. Hearing only static, he hung the phone up.

"Trick 'r Treat," he flatly joked, and she stared at him.

"At least I know it's not you," she sighed, a smile returning to her face as he hugged her. "Back there, that night, have you thought

156

about what your answer would have been?" She asked, studying his face for a response.

"I don't know. I mean—I don't really think it matters, does it?" he responded calmly, preferring to avoid the topic.

"Probably not," she replied, as the volume of the television caught their attention.

The cartoon had concluded and was replaced with local news, running a light-hearted teaser on the fast-growing story of the 'gateway to hell', promising a live news broadcast from the location, followed by a brief montage of lined up cars, rowdy crowds, police lights, and church picketers.

An annoying commercial jingle quickly replaced the advert, and before Robin could change the channel, the phone rang again. This time Robin didn't interfere when Brett motioned to answer, and he picked up the handset, pleased to hear his mom on the other end. Robin appeared relieved as well, as his mother relayed the message that a 'Shea' had called and left his number, which he took down with a pen and paper Robin provided.

Brett explained to Robin how he'd been trying to get in touch with Shea, before dialing his number, noticing Robin handling the small crucifix that hung around her neck. "Hello, Shea?"

"Hey Brett! Did you see the news? I can't believe it... all from some crap I made up!" Shea exclaimed.

"Wait—what... you what?" Brett stuttered.

"Yeah, I made the whole thing up, or most of it," Shea laughed.

Brett covered the mouthpiece. "He says he made the whole thing up," he relayed to a now puzzled Robin, who asked about the name.

"Tuefel? I just said devil with a weird accent; I guess she heard

German… I mean, I knew about that hole for years. I always wondered what was down there, and man, that flare of yours was just the special effect it needed! When you and your girlfriend got freaked out, it only freaked out my friends more. Man, we should've sold tickets," Shea marveled.

"Hang on, someone's at the door," said Shea.

"Huh, that's weird. UHH AHHHH…" Shea bellowed.

"Real funny Shea. More jokes," Brett shook his head and rolled his eyes, waiting. "Shea, that's fun and all, but I'm going to hang up soon."

Brett heard the phone clicking, some scratchy static and a raspy sound. A voice that was not Shea's finally spoke, very slowly and dry, like dead leaves crackling.

"WHAT'S… YOUR… NAME?"

Brett was speechless. A slow loud knock came at Robin's door and she walked to the foyer to answer it, interrupted by Brett.

"Robin! Don't open that!" She turned to face Brett, her eyes widening as he rushed over to her, dropping the phone.

"Who's there!?" Brett shouted through the door, stepping back as Robin recoiled further. The knocking at the door stopped, and from the other side of the door, raspy and scratchy and very wrong… Brett heard the SAME voice from the phone.

"WHAT'S… YOUR… NAME?"

"What the hell is that?" Robin screamed, as scratching sounds could be heard around the outside of the walls, skittering overhead to the roof.

Black soot fell to the hearth as SCRATCHING could be heard

COMING DOWN the chimney, and this time from the fireplace came the voice:

"AND...

ARE...

YOU...

AFRAID?"

About the Author:

Brandon Humphreys' first job was delivering the Akron Beacon Journal newspaper, where he saved enough money to purchase an Atari 2600. More recently he has spent the last 23 years making video games in Southern California.

He still enjoys hiking in Ohio.

Made in the USA
Coppell, TX
28 September 2021